Royal Magic Book 1

Dominique Pryor

Published by Dominique Pryor, 2018.

Table of Contents

Please enjoy.

Table of Content

Prologue

In the Kingdom of Perta, the land of agriculture and farming, stands a castle of white brick with five towers overlooking the city. The capital is called Helena where people of diverse backgrounds gather within the wall of the castle's ground to sell their creations.

These creations vary maker to maker. One is a woman who makes clothes with a needle that moves by itself. Another is a man that makes jewelry just by the flick of his hand. Yes, witchcraft made this city into one of the richest in the kingdom. In the castle in the furthest tower I reside in a room in complete disarray. This room has decorations of colorful paintings of wild animals and pixies all over the white walls.

This room is designed to house the little nobles that will one day rule. Plush pillows, cozy blankets, if you can imagine it, they had it. Five little ones are now trampling over each other and on the many toys that litter the floor. Screaming in glee without a care in the world. And in the corner, trying to read a book, is me; wishing I had not volunteered to watch these rascals today. "Give it back, Roland!" Annie, who has the lungs of a stork, screams.

The little boy in question is holding a small colorful ball away from his companion.

"No, it's mine!" Roland sticking out his tongue and making the girl furious.

"That's it! I'm going to get you!"

The girl gives chase, and the boy runs away like the little troublemaker he is. Distracted, he misses the blocks scattered around the playroom and comes tumbling down. The deafening sound of the fall made me finally get up from my comfortable chair.

Leaving my chair, I feel my aching knees sing. Walking toward the children. I can't help but miss my younger body as I wiggle my legs to ease my cramps. I walk by a mirror and see my appearance.

An old woman in her sixties with graying red hair is staring back at me. I am the spitting image of my Grandma Ruth sixty years ago. I admit, I look fabulous, but I wouldn't mind being that seventeen-year-old girl again in Weston. Now, I am Grandma Ruth, every day in the mirror, and remembering those days were behind me. As I am pouting over my lost youth, my delightful charges knock over the potted plants in the room while chasing each other.

Sighing, I wish again, I hadn't agreed to watch these hell-raisers today.

"What's going on?" I ask with my hands on my hips, taking in the scene before me. Hearing my voice, Roland and Annie turn their heads to me. Twin guilty expressions met my gaze. And my other charges, Micah and the twins are ready to tattle.

I am about to interrogate my other charges when Roland suddenly wails. Lifting himself from the floor, he runs into my knees, almost knocking me to the ground.

Groaning from the impact, I rub the boy's head and smile at my grandson. Yes, Roland is a zealous child who reminds me of myself. *God bless my father for his patience* back then I praised silently.

"Roland, what happened?" I ask, giving him my best stern stare. The aspect I loved about getting older was learning how to intimidate with just a look.

Gulping, Roland tries to tell his version of the story, but I hold up my hand.

"And no lying because Grandma's eyes know it all." I point to my gleaming orbs, and, just to make a point, I use a little of my magic to make them glow. That did the trick because Roland is blabbing on how their disagreement began. He and Annie were playing with watercolors and she decided it was boring. Instead she starts playing with the ball. Roland didn't want to play with the ball and snatched it away.

"Roland, it isn't good to fight with your friends. Now, go apologize to Annie."

He protests, but with my famous glance, the little boy goes over to Annie. Annie with her hands folded in front of her body waiting for his apology. Her stance and mannerism reminds me so much of her grandmother, Rachel. One of the most wonderful friends I ever had in my life. It still hurt knowing that she passed away only a couple of years ago. However Annie is her replica down to her chocolate skin and the shape of her mouth.

Looking at the children, I can see all my friends in their faces. Laura's smile in Micah, her grandson, and the twins had Sarah's brown hair and eyes. Remembering them leaves me with a feeling of sadness. Today would have been the anniversary of Weston being gone, and only half of us remain to mourn. Feeling the tears bloom in my eyes, I picture myself in Weston, laughing and trying to figure out life and boys in the fields of our old home.

"Aunt Andy, why are you crying?" Micah question, my quietest charge. Laura, his grandma insisted we all be aunts, saying that we were practically family and tied at the hip.

I try to put on a smile for Micah because the boy is a wizard. And one of the magical gifts he'd inherited from his grandmother, Laura. Micah can always sense different feelings, which makes hiding things from the child difficult.

With bright blue eyes and dimples for days, Micah is the kindest of his playmates. He is always ready to cheer anyone up and the peacemaker in the group. Especially when my Roland and Annie get into one of their moods.

"I am good, just being a silly, old woman," I laugh, wiping the tears from my face. Micah frowned at my answer but didn't question me further. The last two of my charges make their presence known. Twin girls by the names of Marie and Mary come to me with their matching clothes and pigtailed hair.

"Aunt Andy, we want to hear a story!" Both girls' shouts get the attention of Annie and Roland who appear to have made up. Both of them were worse than Rachel and I when we were younger.

"Yeah, tell us a story about dragons!" Roland yells jumping up and down, from either excitement or the slice of cake I foolishly let him have earlier.

"No, we want princesses," Mary says, with Marie agreeing with her sister. The other children begin to argue about what kind of story they want. However my Micah, the diplomat like his grandmother, proposes a solution.

"Guys, why don't Aunt Andy tell us how she and our grandmothers became the Witches of Weston?" He suggests with the other children nodding in agreement. Holding back a moan I attempt not to let my displeasure show.

"Hey, guys," Trying to think of an alternative to my story. "Let's go outside, I think Navarro is showing off his animals and you all enjoy that." Thinking of the Native wizard who can speak to animals, the children enjoyed him to death. I hope they will agree, but their little heads shake in disagreement.

"No, we want the story."

"Come on, don't you want to play with some toys or take a nap?" I try persuasion, but five tiny scowls is what I receive. Sighing, I know when I am beaten.

"Fine, but Grandma is getting comfortable if she is telling this story. It's very long." I mumble walking back to my rocking chair, and ignoring the squeals of their tiny voices as they follow. Sometimes, watching children can be very tiring.

My rocking chair is in the children's library. My quiet little corner of the room is the only place not filled with toys. I wave at the servants picking up the mess their young master's created.

I shake my head at how good these children had it compared to me at their age. I remember my mother, Ella, making me at four, clean our house; I was her personal servant. I frown, thinking of that woman, it always brings me back to a hard time in my life. One where I remember I only had the love of one parent, and the hatred of the other.

Looking around the room, it astonishes me that these squirts want to hear my old stories. I wait as the children grab pillows and blankets to get cozy on the floor. When they are ready, and giving me their undivided attention, I begin.

"My story, and that of your grandmothers', is a humble one because we didn't grow up in luxury like you have, my dears. I was never a girl who liked fancy things, but I became introduced to them at the end of my tale." I said, looking at the ruby necklace that is gleaming around my neck and the expensive silk dress that cost more than some people earned in a lifetime.

A far cry from the girl who had felt uncomfortable with anything other than an old shirt and pants. I was an odd duck in my younger years, taking my father's old clothes and mending them to fit me. As a girl in Perta, it wasn't the norm, but I didn't care.

I take in a deep breath as the memories come rushing back to me. "I grew up in the cornfields with good people and great friends I will always hold dear to me. And that is where my journey starts, in a place I loved dearly and miss very much, Weston.

Weston

The heat is blistering and the sun shines brightly today. Shielding my eyes with my hands isn't keeping the sun at bay so I can finish my task. Of course, being in the middle of a cornfield among endless ears of yellow with no shade isn't helping either. My untrainable red curls stuck to me like a second skin. I had sweated more today than I ever had in the seventeen years I'd been alive.

What a sight I must be, I thought. I could hear my mother's condescending tone in my head.

"Andy, you look like a pig," she would say with a snotty voice, sliding her hands through her perfectly straight blond hair that I didn't inherit. My mother, Ella, wanted her daughters to always look perfect.

Her motto is to look your best to gain the attention of men. As her daughter, I'm told I am a disappointment for not living up to her ideals. Instead of trying to make me bend to her will, she just focuses on my older sister and lets my father raise me. It was like having one parent and Ella only acknowledged me if the fields needed tending.

Honestly the fields are all the villagers responsibility to handle. Our village is a shared community that profits off the land and the products we grow. Every villager is accountable for their share of work in the crops. But somehow, Ella got out of her share of the work by making me do it.

Thinking about it always makes me miserable. Ignoring my increasing anger, I pick up another piece of corn, attempting to finish my task before dinner, which I must prepare. Ella, and my sister refuse to prepare food. They feel it is beneath them to have to make dinner, that it is a job for a servant meaning me.

I wonder what it would be like to have a family that helps each other, but it isn't meant to be. To them, I did not have their beauty, and would be better off doing menial tasks.

I wish one day to be the girl who is proper and beautiful. The girl who the whole village looks upon in wonder.

I snort at the thought I can't be proper even if it was my name. I am just a beanpole of a girl who isn't good at anything, and everyone knows it. Being stuck in the cornfield is a blessing. At least here, it felt like I am making a difference, even a small one.

A few more minutes pass by of me picking corn with one hand and shielding the elements with another. Until a giant speck of dirt gets in my eyes, burning them profusely. Rubbing and attempting to remove the unwanted invader from them. I trip on my pant's leg, falling on my bottom.

I groan in pain, but the noise is overshadowed by the cruel laughter of my sister, Mel. Great, the one person who had to see me fall is my sister. Wincing, I turn around and prepare for whatever rude remark my sister is going to fling my way. She is lounging on the ground, using her magic to make the dirt around her swirl like a mini tornado. My mouth drops, at my sister's attitude and the injustice of it all.

I'm sweating like a hog in the summer while Mel is acting like this is a holiday. Our mother sent us both to do the crops. Like usual, while I did the work by myself, Mel slacks off. Who was I kidding, thinking this day would be any different? This had been the routine since we were small. Mel believes that her job is to be pampered, while I did the hard labor. She even told me so in that arrogant tone of hers as she left her share of work on my shoulders.

"Andy, you should be happy, I'm giving you practice for what you will be doing for the rest of your life." She said when we were ten and twelve years of age. For some reason Mel and I couldn't get along. We were sisters and close in age but every time I tried to get closer to her; she would block

8

my efforts. And after what she said on that day, we would never have a chance to be real siblings.

"It is beneath me to work in the fields. I will be a lady someday and need to conserve my beauty." Mel said, while brushing her hair and giving me a cruel smile. "Hey, you might even catch a husband in one of the field hands. When they see what a strong worker you are, your lack of beauty will not be a factor." And with that she left our shared room.

That comment had affected me, and Mel knew it. She always bullies me about my natural appearance. My wild hair and lack of curves that other girls my age are developing. Our mother, Ella, even agrees with Mel and goes so far as to join in with Mel's taunting when father isn't home.

Ella is my mother by blood and birth but I could never call her that in my head. That woman, in all my memories, never has shown me any motherly affection. It's always mean comments or shunning me for Mel.

She even told me at the age of eight. That the name Andy was intended for the son my parents dreamed of having, but instead they got worthless me. I remember crying myself to sleep that night and only getting up because of my father. He told me it wasn't true, and Ella lied that he always wanted me.

Even though I hated hearing that from Ella, I am proud of my name. Andy sounds strong, and it honors my father, Andrew, a Weston council member and the village leader. Knowing that father is so respected made me stand taller and love the name Andy even more.

I must have been daydreaming because a small pebble hit me square in the forehead making me wince. Looking where the rock comes from I find Mel glaring at me. "What is the matter with you? That could have hurt me Mel." I scream out checking for blood on my forehead. Seeing none, I breathe a sigh of relief.

"As if that ugly face of yours could get any worse." Mel snaps back giving me a cold smile making me want to hit her. Holding myself back knowing father didn't want us to fight anymore.

Our last fight ended with Mel and me having to clean out the barn as he supervised us. It wasn't a pleasant experience shoveling dung from the horses, even if Mel looked ready to faint from the smell.

Taking a breather, I knew if I didn't say anything. It would be a more significant blow to Mel's ego than a punch to her perfect face. And being the predictable sister, Mel's face starts to turn red at my quietness giving me a small victory. She stands up trying to look tough but only makes herself look constipated. Smiling, I can't be happier with my unruly curls which conceals my merriment at my sister's expense.

"Hurry up, Andy." My sister orders pulling on her cascading blond curls. "Mother hates it when you make us late for dinner!" I bit back a retort about helping me knowing that it will backfire in my face, as Ella always takes Mel's side. Scratching my head in frustration, I thought of what my grandmother told me about turning a situation into your favor.

I might not be able to get Mel to help me physically in the cornfield. Although I can mention I am not happy with the dust, which she can do something about. Yet I must word it right, my sister will never help me unless it benefits herself.

"Well," I shrug trying to sound nonchalant. "If you send the dust packing. I can see the corn stalks more clearly and get done quicker." Rolling her blue eyes at the comment, she continues ignoring me. Realizing Mel is not taking the bait, I add something to sweeten the pot. "You can go home and discuss with our mother what you will wear to the festival if I finish quicker." And with that my sister's eyes spark to life and with a flick of her wrist, the dust scatters to the four winds. I have to hide a smile, so Mel can't see how happy I am. Sometimes it pays to have a sister who has magic over the earth, even if it gives her an even bigger ego than she already possesses.

Mel is what people call an earth witch, possessing the power to control minerals and the growth of crops. Only four witches in our small village possess the power, which made Mel an asset to our home.

Our town Weston is small compared to the other nearby cities, but it's fertile. A speck in the vast Kingdom of Perta. Yet Weston's crops had given Queen Katherine the power to make treaties with twenty different nations who are benefitting from our plants. Famed for its green, fertile lands, people refer to Perta as the "Gold Land," and Weston is in the center of it.

Its bounty has ensured Perta a peace for more than three decades. We the villagers rely on that income because our main profit is crops and Mel's powers assist with that. Knowing this, my sister often walks around like she is a queen and the villagers worship her as one.

I shudder, remembering that possibility can come true. Recently Queen Katherine had departed this world leaving her unwedded son the throne. Mel, god help her, is the most selfish person I know and would make a horrible leader.

Only a few people are immune to Mel's attitude and see through her ruses. Her behavior embarrasses me, as she treats people as though they aren't worthy to be in the same space as her.

Groaning, I acknowledge how people are misled into believing her. My sister had some redeeming features that I don't. With white skin, pale blue eyes, and long blond hair, straight from our mother, and her hourglass figure. Which helps to make the village men susceptible to her charms. Standing next to her I feel like an ogre, not her sister.

My friend Rachel, who must be blind, said that I couldn't see the charm in my red curls. My breasts are small, but my lithe figure still causes some men to give me a second look. Even though I try to hide it in baggy shirts and pants my figure is still visible.

My clothing choice isn't what girls my age wear, but I don't feel comfortable in dresses. Spending most of my time in the fields, it didn't make sense to get dolled up. Besides, someone has to feed the family, since Ella or Mel won't.

My tanned skin, bright red curls, and hazel eyes are my most becoming features. They aren't common characteristics around these parts. And lastly, a skill, unique to me, is my magical power of foresight which makes all the villagers worship me as a goddess.

At my own joke, I chuckle as I fill my basket with more ears of corn. The villagers think my magic is a joke. "What good was foresight?" they say, compared to my sister's power? And I must agree telling the future is what fortune tellers do in the traveling shows that pass through Weston. Grandma Ruth, who also has the gift, said to me that my visions will someday show me essential people and places that will affect the future of my life.

So far, my visions have been unremarkable and a complete letdown. And they haven't won me any unique standing with the villagers who see me as Mel's useless sister.

Groaning at my lack of usefulness. I focus on filling the basket with corn and shift my thoughts to the upcoming Princess Festival and the royals who would be attending. The event brings a smile to my face at last, just thinking of the fun I can have.

The Princess Festival is held every five years. It is the main way that Princes looking for a witch bride finds one to marry. The purpose is for the royals to choose a wife of common birth and magical heritage to help their nation. The idea is to show the people in their country that their ruler can understand their troubles. And the best way of showing that is to marry a commoner. Someone who can relate to their problems and can be their voice.

And a witch is the best choice, since they can use their magic to aid their new husband's kingdom. The unmarried royals visits every village participating in the festival until they find their witch bride. The witches have no choice but to marry the prince who selects them unless they are already engaged. My friends and I hate this rule. I just can't see myself submitting to marriage with a stranger! However the festival has games, food and singing; a good time for all.

Still, two months remain until the festival. Feeling the pressure of all I have to do to help Weston be ready. Father put me in charge of decorations and food, giving me a headache. My eyes squint, taking my sister humming to herself braiding corn stalks into her hair. I pray a prince will remove her lazy behind from my life soon.

"Done," I huff, tossing one last corn ear into the basket.

"It's about time," Mel growls. "With those manly arms, you should be quicker!" and with that nice remark. My sister gracefully rises to her feet and starts for home. Leaving me to shoulder the full weight of the basket filled with corn. Sparing her another glare, I struggle to lift the hamper which feels like half my load is bearing down on my shoulders.

Only then did I look at the thirty or so men who occupy the field with me and feel sad. These men are local farmers or old soldiers' marching with rusted swords and pitchforks. Ready to lay down their lives if necessary, to protect the crops.

I look to the far east of our field for the reason why. Beyond the green of the current crops are the empty blackness of scorched earth. Once fifty acres, the crop fields were now down to thirty acres, following recent raids by the neighboring kingdom, Deliania.

Deliania and our village used to have a steady peace, but the Delianians King was assassinated by his enemies. Having no direct heir, those looking to sit on his throne now desire to take Weston's valuable lands. Weston was a once peaceful place where people did not fear going to work, but those days are gone.

Every day we see our fields gone and men are killed to protect our livelihood. Now fewer crops were produced, and funerals are becoming a common occurrence.

War is such a waste, but there's nothing I can do about it. We only have two hopes for saving our crops. The first is to pray the Delianians get tired of damaging our fields. The second is to get professional soldiers to help us fight; but both were unlikely. We have less money than before and what we do have is being spent on the festival to impress the Royals. Weston only has retired soldiers and youthful men who can barely swing a sword to fight.

Shaking my head at the disheartening situation, I move to leave only to stop again. Blocking my path is Mel and several young guards who are supposed to be on duty. Instead they are fawning over my sister, forgetting the reason they were here. I guess protecting our livelihood wasn't as important as getting a pretty girl's attention.

Grunting, what did I expect? Most of the guards were only a couple of years older than Mel and myself. One persistent young man named Luke, a local blacksmith apprentice, hands Mel a sunflower. Leaning forward and giving a sly smile, Luke is a natural charmer.

"Melissa, would you be so kind as to accompany me to the local pub for a drink today." Luke flirts, making Mel giggle at his proposal. Rolling my eyes, I watch Luke slide his hands down her back and come to rest on her bottom. Batting his hands away Mel only chuckles at his daring action.

"I would like to, Luke " My sister refuse sweetly. " But I was picking corn all day by my lonesome without help from my useless sister." The accusation with a pout had their stares turn to me completely missing Mel's smirk of satisfaction. My face turns red at my sister's lie as many hateful eyes glare at me.

"That's a lie." Defending myself but it is of no use. When Mel says something, people eat it up even if it's a lie. Even though I did all the work and carried the basket. The men will still take her side just because she's Mel.

Luke, one of her numerous followers, comes straight to her aid. "How could you do this to her Andy? After all that she does for the village with her magic." As if that gives her a free pass I thought. Nevertheless I keep my mouth shut knowing these idiots will not listen to logic.

"She's just jealous that Melissa's power is greater than hers." One of the young guards comments sneering at me. And just like that, they poked the bear, and my temper is my worst flaw.

My biggest trigger is when people call me envious of my sister. Which might be a little true, but no one better say it to my face. Slamming the basket of corn on the ground, I march up to those morons who are fawning over Mel. The lovesick boys tower over me which should have intimidated me, but I inherited my Father's red hair and boldness.

"If I am jealous of anything about my sister. It's her ability to make simpletons believe her falsehoods, not her magic."

"We aren't simpletons" Luke shouted out upset at my accusation.

"Well, Luke explain this." I ask pointing at my sweat covered shirt and pants. "Why are my clothes dirty and Mel's look perfectly clean if she did all the work?" At my proof the naysayers have no answers and with that, I walk away leaving Mel to her admirers.

I refuse to deal with this now, and the walk home always calms me down.

I'm almost out of the field when I hear a voice call out to me. Turning around one of the older guards is coming towards me. Feeling tense, I'm not ready for another verbal attack, but he surprises me. "Don't let those fools get you down. They are just blinded by a pretty face and cannot see what a true gem looks like." The man says patting me on the back and returning to his post.

My mouth is open, but I close it and return to my walk. Maybe some men aren't as dumb about my sister's faults as I once believed. Grinning, I reach the fields and take in the sights in front of me. Flowers from daisies, wildflowers, and sunflowers in bloom surrounding the pastures that scatter the landscape. Hill after hills are on display around me, and I can't help feeling proud to call Weston home. Just above the village gate on top of the hill overlooking Weston is the red cobblestone house that is my home. Seeing it, I'm relieved. Maybe I finally could get some well-deserved sleep and a bite to eat.

Mothers and Daughters

❚❚ A little sleep and a bite to eat was too much to hope for with these ingrates. "I mumble chopping up some onions ignoring the endless ranting of my so-called family. Mel and Ella are like queens sitting in the kitchen laughing while I'm forced to be their servant. And just as I think of that remark here comes Ella's condescending voice.

"Andy, hurry up, we are hungry over here." She demands while braiding Mel's hair something my mother will never do for me. Biting back my tongue I get to work again wondering how I ended up with a mother like Ella. Ella is a mean-spirited woman who takes pleasure in another's unhappiness.

"Yeah back to work, ogre," Mel says looking at her braided hair in the mirror. Rolling my eyes, I try to pretend those words didn't bother me much. They did though luckily Ella and Mel are so engrossed in their world. My emotions escapes their notice as they discuss their hair and outfits for the festival.

"Momma do you think a prince will like my hair this way?" Mel puffing up her perfect curls while glancing at the small mirror Ella is holding up.

"Honey you will be the brightest star at the festival. No prince could deny such a beauitful girl like yourself.".

"Really momma."

"Yes, Melissa, you have beauty and power. Things that your useless waste of a sister doesn't have." Ella says, looking at me when she utters those words. I don't flinch trying to be silent hoping the bullying will stop. And like always my prayers are not granted as they surround me

"Yeah, Andy will be lucky to get a pig farmer to marry her." Mel gives me a once over in disgust. "Look at her she cannot even make her hair presentable, but fortunately pigs are as ugly as her. Imagine the poor man having to sleep with something more hideous than the animals he slaughters."

"Melissa, even pigs have some beauty. Andy's only choice is a blind man, if your father can find one" Ella comments cruelly.

"Good one Mother" Mel laughs with Ella giggling beside her.

Feeling the familiar rise of anger in me, I try to focus on my task at hand. If I can get done with dinner then I can go to my room until father gets home. Ella and Mel are less nasty with him there. Nonetheless you can tell the two have no love for my father, especially Ella.

My parent's relationship is that of two strangers living in the same house. They never kiss or show affection. I sometimes wonder how Mel and myself were born. My suspicion is that my parents' marriage was arranged like many others in Weston. Rumor has it that my mother's parents wanted their daughter married to the future Weston leader. And Ella is a weather witch that can control the elements. That was a benefit to Weston; one I knew my father wouldn't pass up.

Sighing, I change topic and thought of the festival again. The Princess Festival is coming up in two more months, and the village needs more preparations. Banners and decorations need to be hung, and the food needs to be perfect. Since the invaders have come, many of the villager's fear for the future. With no aid from our new sovereign of Perta, Weston is on its own and father is at his wits end.

"Mother, do you think father will let me have the blue velvet dress we saw in Ms. Clara's store yesterday?" Mel asks, hopping up and down. I bit my tongue. There is no way Father will let her have that dress. It cost ten gold coins; that's enough to feed our family for two months.

" I can talk that buffoon into anything" Ella scoffs, twirling her blond curls. "A woman can always talk a man into anything with the right assets" gesturing to her breasts. "Melissa, remember that when you snag a prince, " Listening to them I roll my eyes at that remark. If a prince could be tricked by that then he is an idiot.

"Mother, Father only cares about this horrible village and saving it. He doesn't care about me getting a prince" Mel throwing a fit. "Father is stupid, and I wish he would just let this village burn to the ground."

And with that I had enough. These women can talk about me all they want, but Father and the village are off limits.

Throwing down the knife I am using. I march right up to Mel and Ella giving them the defiant look. "Without this horrible village," I mimic her voice. "You wouldn't even have a chance to meet a prince."

The rage that I built up is gone and my blond family members are furious at my display of disobedience.

"Get out of my face" yelped Mel, pushing me back a few steps." Weston is a useless village that is about to burn around us. And I for one don't feel Father should waste his time trying to save it."

"Weston can be saved. Father says with the festival we might get help." I insist knowing that was my father's main goal with the festival.

"You are a bigger fool than Father" Mel laughs.

"I am no fool to have hope neither is Father. If his plan works Weston, with different royals on our side, can finally hire a militia and fight the Delianians properly." I explain knowing this was our village's best chance at survival. My father works endlessly trying to make sure everyone has enough to eat and to make sure the crops are protected. However his efforts are in vain because the patrol and guards cannot keep the Delianians out.

I am about to go on when cackling from Ella made me stop. "What's so funny?" I frown, getting annoyed that Ella, the village leader's wife, can be so cold. How can she not see how important this festival is to father and our village. It's not just for Mel and herself to plot their plans to become royals.

"You sound just like your father Andy, as foolish and naïve as he is." Ella says, giving me a look of annoyance. "He believes that the Royal's will care about this little village when our own ruler has given up on us."

Hearing those words from her mouth makes my worst thoughts feel like a reality. It's true, countless letters have been sent to the capital Helena. And we have not received a response from the king.

"There is always hope" a booming voice says coming from the door. Hearing that voice makes me relax as my father in his six-foot three glory walks into the room. His hazel eyes look tired from a long day of work, but still has a sharpness to them. "Hope is something that is never foolish or irrational to have".

"It is when we know the outcome, Andrew" Ella hiss, putting her hands on her hips, stubbornly. "It is time for you to give up and focus on Melissa getting married. She can be seen by the royals and is our best chance of becoming somebody". As she says these words, Mel puffs up in pride. "Look at her, Andrew, she is made to be a princess and live in luxury. How could you deny your daughter that?"

And with that, Ella's voice turns sweet trying to trick my father with her charms. Yet father is aware of her cunning as he leans against the table. Taking a good look at Mel, he gives a kind smile. Although the stare when it lands on Ella changes.

"I care, Ella, but I think you are missing something," Father says coldly.

"What am I missing?"

"Andy can participate too, or have you forgotten your other daughter." Father lifting his eyebrow waiting for a response. I know my father is only standing up for me, but he always ends up making it worse.

"Of course not." Ella claims, giving me a glance before she says anything else. And judging by her expression what she sees isn't pleasing. "Let's put our best foot forward with Melissa first. Andy isn't beautiful and can be manlier than you at times" she says in a dismissive tone. Missing father's angry face at her callousness. I gesture to him, showing him, I am not bothered by the statement. I don't want Father fighting with Ella, it never gets anywhere. She will still hate me and favor Mel, that's our family.

Snorting, I go back to the table to finish cutting the vegetables when Father speaks again. "Andy, can you be a Dear and deliver a message to Tim Walker for me?" Taking a seat next to me, I feel dread instantly. Grimacing at the name because where Tim Walker is located so is his son, Matthew. The boy who thinks he fancies me.

"Father, please don't make me go" I beg looking at him but only getting a stern look in return. I know that glance. My father's mind is made up and there was no changing it. Going over to him, I saw him write something on a piece of paper and seal it in an envelope. Leaning in to grab the letter, Father whispers in a voice only we can hear.

"Take a break from here" he says, giving me a kind look. "Once you deliver the message go visit Sarah and Rachel. They both should be done with their work and I'll finish dinner." Switching places with me, father takes the knife away and starts chopping vegetables.

" Dad" I mumble, feeling bad that he is finishing dinner after a hard day of work. He stubbornly pushes me to the door. With that, Father gives me a gentle kiss on my forehead and a beaming smile that lit up his tan face. "Go, I think you had a worse day than me dealing with your mother's harping." He whispers scowling at Ella and Mel as they forget we are in the room.

Trying to keep my joy about leaving contained, I squeeze my father's hand giving him a quick kiss. I'm out of the door in seconds running from the house. I try not to shout in happiness until I know I am out of hearing range.

Father is a genius, the Walker's house is right in-route to my two best friend's homes. After delivering the letter, I will have free time to chat with them.

Walking down the hill of my house I can see the road that leads into Weston and the fields surrounding it. Weston is majestic in the daytime; it's like living inside a watercolor painting. The view keeps my mind off the meeting that will come from the Walker's residence.

Matthew Walker has been enamored with me since I turned fifteen two years ago. Many girls in my position would be happy to have a young man showing them attention. Especially someone like Matthew, who has blond haired, muscular shoulders and strong chisel chin. Matthew is a catch in looks alone, but he's also a bully.

He is known to torment the less wealthy in Weston. One of those people is my friend, Sarah, the sweetest girl in the village. Just because her clothes aren't new, and she has to work at the local inn doesn't mean Sarah is less worthy. And if this is the man that shows interest in me, then I'm dying to be an old maid.

I'm optimistic about this trip because of my friends Rachel and Sarah. Finally, someone to talk to who doesn't insult my clothes or hair. Unfortunately the only downside is that Laura, my other best friend, cannot be here. She and her father have business with another Native tribe.

Nearing the village entrance, I hear a sharp whistling sound slicing through the air. Turning around I find the source of the sound. A large group of travelers at the eastern end of the village engulfs everything around them. Scanning the crowd, I count thirty men all carrying weapons. Looking at the group I notice most of the men wearing armor but two are in plainclothes.

I take a closer look at the two strangers. Both men look to be in their early twenties and each handsome in their own way. One man has pale skin with dark hair and eyes that offset his high cheekbones. What got me the most, was the pleasant smile he sends to curious onlookers that swarm them. In comparison, his companion looks rigid with the attention they are getting.

His forest green eyes were alert and looked ready to draw the sword that is attached to his side. He is like a fish out of water standing there, and the scowls he is throwing made onlookers flinch. I can't blame them, the man had to be six feet tall and with a muscular build that people only see on soldiers. His dark brown hair was cut short but has a shagginess that I like.

I shake my head. I can't believe I thought that. This man isn't cute, and I certainly didn't like him even if he did have the most glorious green eyes I ever seen. Against my better judgment, I steal another glance and come face to face with those green eyes. Holding back a surprised gasp, I saw the stranger is handsomer now than before. His stern face seems to be taking me in and he is not in any hurry to stop.

Blushing, I feel myself trying to brush the tangles from my hair. I must have looked like a horrid sight to behold. Pulling my eyes away is harder than I thought but when I did my composure was back.

I decide to go directly to the Walker house, so I can deliver Father's message. Going down the path, I jump when a hand touches my shoulder. Holding back a shriek, I spun around ready to give whoever that scared me a piece of my mind. Yet the gentle smile of the first stranger halts that.

Holding up his hand in apology "Sorry to frighten you, Miss, but someone told me you could help me." The man says with a sultry accent that would make women swoon.

" How can I help you?" I am a little shocked that this man is actually talking to me.

"Someone mentioned that you might know where Andrew Miller is located. " The man responds to me in a patient voice.

"What business do you have with my father?" I blurt out, feeling my face turn red getting the attention of his friend who comes up.

"It is none of your concern now, answer my friend's question." says the green-eyed man. His voice makes my skin flush despite the rudeness in his tone. Shaking my head, I try to get this silly flutter out of my stomach. I have to stay focused and not fantasize about how good this man's voice sounds.

"It is, since I handle most of my father's day to day business." I reply harshly back without meaning offense, and it makes both men laugh at my response. My temper rises more because of their laughter. My face turns red the only indicator I'm angry but the first man noticed my emotions shifting..

"We're sorry my dear but no one ever corrects Jacob like that because of his status." The first man remarks pointing to the green eyed Jacob who was still laughing. I didn't catch the last part until late but when I did I grew anxious.

"What do you mean by status?" I respond, already knowing the answer. Straightening his posture, the man's whole demeanor changes.

"Beg your pardon Miss, I forgot my manners," the man says in a formal voice." I am Prince Mark of Gallopia, and this is Jacob of Polla" motioning to his friend as both men bow. The entire village hears their introduction and we are now the center of attention. I can't blame them; Gallopia and Polla are well-known Kingdoms and very wealthy nations.

"It can't be. You weren't supposed to arrive for two months" I squeak out.

"We have business that couldn't wait and came to talk to your father about it." Jacob answers with a slightly amused smirk.. As he spoke the stranger did something unexpected and pushed my curls behind my ear, earning a blush from me. Is this man flirting with me? Although the next thing that comes out of his mouth destroys that notion.

"So, fire head, can you help us?" he remarks liking my dumbfounded expression. My temper begins to rise and a thought comes to my head. Why are all good-looking people jerks?

Swallowing the words that wanted to come out of my mouth, I remember father's urgent business and his plans for the royals. Weston's perils must come first before my anger. It's time to act like the lady Ella always desired.

I am about to curtsy when running footsteps interrupted that. Two men that I will recognize for all my life walk up in a hurry. Tim Walker, the man my father sent me to deliver the letter to, is out of breath in his red satin shirt and leather pants.

He looks out of place next to the dirty clothing of the average villager in his attire. Tim is always dressed to impress and has shown that in his fifty eight years of life. Next to him is Cody Walker, Tim's oldest son, a man in his twenties.

I am cheering in my head when I can't see Matthew, the last of the Walkers. Finally, some deity is looking out for me.

"Mr. Walker, what can we do for you?" I ask but they just ignore me and go straight for the Royals.

"Welcome to Weston, your Highnesses," Tim says, bowing with a friendly smile that didn't reach his eyes.

My grandmother always told me someone's eyes can tell you a lot about them. And Tim's shows he is plotting something. Feeling the hairs go up on my neck, I hope the Royals can handle him.

It seems Jacob caught on to it too as he frowns at Tim not fooled in the least.

"Thank you for your greeting, but I didn't get your names," Prince Mark replies the gentlemen of the two.

"Of course, Where are my manners? I am Tim Walker, and this is my son Cody." Motioning to Cody as his son begins to move forward with a hint of pride. He resembles a goose who just got their feathers plucked by the way he walks up. I snicker at the idea, earning the attention of Jacob.

"Mark, we forgot to get the fire head's name over here." Jacob of Polla points out and Prince Mark looks horrified at the oversight.

"What were we thinking,what's your name, miss." Prince Mark in an apologetic tone.

"It doesn't matter" I mumble trying to reassure him that I wasn't offended but I get interrupted by Tim again.

"The girl's name is Andy, but she is of no importance. Gentlemen, if you have any questions I am sure I am better qualified than this dimwitted girl. Run along Andy, men are handling business." Tim grunts out shoving me and making me stumble to the ground. Mark and Jacob look furious by the action and instantly help me up.

Once I am standing I march up to Tim Walker, my eyes glowing with magic. That dimwitted comment goes too far and being shove he just pissed me off. "I am not stupid, you pompous blowhard" I scream out catching Tim by surprise.

"How dare you speak to me like this little girl. Know your place and curve that awful tongue of yours." Tim yells, his face glowing red with anger.

I am about to give the blowhard another piece of my mind when a sharp pull on my arm yank me off balance. Turning toward the source, I see Cody with an enraged expression on his face.

"Andy, behave yourself like a girl for once and be quiet." Cody tries to scold me before yelping when I elbow him to get out of his grip. Observing my arm, a purple mark appeared on it. Just when I'm about to say something else Cody mentions one more thing that makes me freeze. "You better apologize or Matthew might rethink your marriage, and you'll be an old maid for life."

"What are you talking about, you idiot?"

Lifting an eyebrow Cody looks perplexed. "Your father didn't tell you Matthew asked for your hand in marriage?" Shocked, I put my hand on my heart.

How could father not tell me that knowing my feelings for Matthew. A sting of betrayal fills me but I snap out of it my father wouldn't force me to marry Matthew against my will. That isn't the type of man he is and I believe in the man that raised me.

"My father would never agree to something without my consent." I respond, getting a reaction from Cody that looks like uncertainty." I am right there is no agreement so stop flapping your mouth about this nonsense."

"It is only a matter of time until Andrew lets it happen. You aren't lining up with suitors like Melissa" Cody counters. " Women are made to serve men and once you become Matthew's wife you will behave or be punished."

There was only silence after that. The threat is clear: they will beat me into submission if I become part of that family.

"I wouldn't marry your brother if he was the last man breathing. And I would think it's a personal insult to join your family of pigs" I screech so loud my voice vibrates in my ears.

I must have looked ready to punch Cody because a firm grip pulls me away from him. From the gazes, I'm receiving back, Cody is also ready to swing. Turning around I realize the grip that pulled me away is Mark, and he looks at me like I'm going to break. And truthfully, I feel a little overwhelmed at this moment. The marriage thing and the bullying is making me act irrational. Trying to block out sounds to breathe and get my bearing back is impossible. I can hear all the whispers of the villagers around me.

"Andy, that girl is so improper speaking like that to Tim." One woman voices defending the Walkers even after all they said about me. "That one is an embarrassment to the Millers."

I become frozen as the anger rolls away and I listen to the things the villagers are saying. I can see many frowning faces from both women and men in Weston. All looking at me in disgust for the way I talk to Tim. In their eyes, proper young girls speak respectfully to their elders.

"I hope Andy didn't ruin the royal's visit with her behavior and damn us all." One lady comments and the other villagers pipe in. I feel my face redden realizing I just ruined Weston's one shot at getting help.

No royals in their right mind will help a village when the village leader's daughter isn't civilized.

At that moment, I feel like the waste of space Ella always told me I am. I just want to dig a hole and lie in it because this endless rambling was numbing. I slid to the ground and I started to block out everything trying to get at least some peace from this misery.

Rachel and Sarah

Just when I'm about to sink further into despair from the whispers around me. A soulful voice comes to my aid like a saving grace. "Sarah, look at what we found here," says a familiar voice of a black female walking out of the crowd. People move out of her way like she is a battering ram. Standing six-foot-tall, she dwarfs most of the men in our village and towers over the meek brunette that follows behind her.

"Rachel, don't stand there, her shame will get on you" Cody grunts out coming over to stand next to the black female.

"It's just Andy, and she will never be shameful, " Rachel says in defense of me. Ignoring Cody she offers a hand to me. " Time to get off the ground Andy." Pulling me up I am relieved and then quickly mortified when she slaps my butt making me wince.

"Rachel, that hurts" I yell rubbing my butt.

"Good, now no more causing trouble today." Rachel chuckles in humor. Although her mood changes instantly when someone in the crowd says something about my tantrum.

Swinging around, my friend is terrifying when angered, and not just because of her height. With smooth dark brown skin, amber eyes, and a figure that made men drool she is a force of nature, literally.

Rachel is an earth witch like my sister and luckily the attention didn't go to her head making her insufferable. No, she is still the overprotective big sister who will punch someone who went against her loved ones.

"Go away" Rachel snaps at a woman. The woman in question looks scared and shocked at the rage coming from my friend. "Shameful gossipers" my friend growls at another woman who said I am a disappointment making her go white. The woman flees before Rachel could lay into her more. I stand back watching Rachel lecture the crowd to the point people left willingly.

"This is chaos," Sarah stutters out . Jerking at her murky skirt nervously, I can tell Sarah wanted to be anywhere but here as one of the onlookers begins to point at her. Seeing her face fluster from the attention I know I have to do something to ease her nerves.

"Yeah, her nagging is getting worse each day" I joke but can't help but be happy having a friend like Rachel in my corner. Even if you are as guilty as sin, she will have your back. It's one of her greatest gifts and flaws.

My friend's loyalty sometimes blinds her from seeing the truth about a person's character. Looking at Cody Walker shamefully gawking at another girl, with Rachel only feet away. It makes me want to scream at how my friend couldn't see through this creep.

A touch on my shoulder brings my attention back to Sarah. She looks at me with concern "Are you okay, Andy?" Swallowing, I scanned the crowd seeing most of the people were gone.

"Yeah, I'm alright, thanks to you guys." I say, knowing that without my friends this mess would have ended up badly for me.

"I didn't do anything, it was all Rachel's doing." Sarah is surprised when I embrace her. My friend's body is a little rounder than most, but I could always get my arms around her easily.

"You stayed around that's what counts," I answer ignoring Sarah squirming in my grip. Being the naturally reserved one in the group, Sarah hates anything that brought attention, and a public embrace will do that.

"Okay Andy I get it, now release me people are looking." Sarah wheezes a little at how hard I am squeezing her. Loosening my grip a bit but I keep hugging her not wanting to let go.

"There better be hugs for me because I had to yell at a lot of people for you, Andy" Rachel ribs behind us. Laughing Sarah and I let her into the hug. And like that, I blocked out the sounds of everything and enjoyed a moment with my friends.

"Fire head, are you going to introduce us or hug, all day?" Jacob says, interrupting our moment. Rolling my eyes I am forced to release my friends and glower at the royal who ruined our fun.

"Of course, your Highness" I mutter out, only gaining a smirk from Jacob. "These are my best friends Rachel Goodman, and Sarah Palmer".

With that, both of my friends curtsies to the royals. Just as my friends are about to rise, Prince Mark comes forward with a gentle smile. Knowing that look, I wait for the prince to flirt with Rachel, but the royal gives me a big surprise.

"It is a pleasure to meet beautiful ladies such as yourselves" Mark says smoothly striding up to Sarah taking her hand. Rachel and I freeze as he gives her a charming smile. The prince is flirting with her or maybe he is just being polite. Though the next words from his mouth shatter the latter. "Sarah is a lovely name for a gorgeous maiden like yourself."

"Really?" Sarah with disbelief in her voice and I can't blame her. Sarah is what you might call a little rounder in the middle than most girls our age. She has a round face that brings out her green eyes and cute button nose. And with straight brown hair, I wish I had. Sarah in my opinion is beautiful.

In another village she would be considered a catch with being a water witch. However because of her father, Sarah is looked at like scum. John Palmer has single handedly ruined his daughter's status by his behavior as the village drunk and troublemaker.

"Of course, I'm sure many young men tell you the same thing." Mark professes his gleaming smile and Sarah becomes putty in his hands.

"Oh, you don't have to say that."

"Yes, I do. My mother always says "speak honestly".

"Well, tell your mother she raised a gentleman," Sarah says with a blush.

"Maybe you can tell her yourself one day." Mark grins with my friend giggling like a schoolgirl.

I get a sour feeling in my gut watching my friend. Sarah is typically the shyest person I know yet now she is becoming a whole different person. She giggles and laughs at everything Mark says which is getting on my nerves.

"Did he forget about us or did we just become obsolete?" Rachel asks her hands on her hip, apparently not liking what she is seeing either. She looks ready to snatch Sarah away like a mama lion, and I am right along with her.

"I don't like it one bit.".

"What is she doing?" Rachel grumbles to me." Sarah has to know he's a prince and can possibly take her away from us."

And with that Rachel's words pull together my worst fears about the festival. Both Rachel and Sarah are elemental witches. Those powers are what many royals search for magic like theirs to help their kingdoms. It wouldn't be surprising that a royal who requires a water witch picks Sarah.

"No, he cannot take her, and Sarah wouldn't go she wouldn't leave us." I am a little bit afraid. If the prince chooses Sarah. She'll be lost to us forever moving to a new land.

"Andy, you know the law better than me, she will have no choice in the matter." Rachel, reminds me of the law involving witches and the festival. The law states a witch that doesn't have a marriage contract. Must marry the royal that chooses them, or face punishment from their country.

"Maybe she's a passing fancy for him." I mention in a hopeful voice to Rachel, but the response I get back isn't from her.

"Sorry, you're wrong. Mark isn't someone who plays around with emotions, especially with women." Jacob speaks up, making Rachel and I jump in fright.

"How do we know that? Sarah is our friend and we will not let a prince take her away." Rachel hiss staring at Mark and Sarah looking ready to separate them, but a male voice catches her attention.

"Rachel honey, did you forget about me?" Cody calls and instantly Rachel's thoughts about Sarah are gone.

"Of course not dear, now all my attention is on you," She says, coming over to kiss Cody deeply. Rolling my eyes I look away at the display of Rachel being a lovesick puppy when it comes to Cody. She loves him deeply and would do anything for him which he didn't deserve.

Cody, I know, isn't loyal to Rachel and courts women behind her back. I have informed Rachel of that fact but she will not believe me saying I am mistaken. Remembering such a time I told her about his activities.

Andy, it's a lie Cody loves me and wouldn't do this" she shouts.

That day, Rachel and I had one of the biggest fights in our friendship over the relationship. She stopped speaking to me for weeks. We only became friends again because Laura, the diplomat in our group, made us. Threatening to tell all our secrets if we did not make up.

"Well, your friend is easily distracted," Jacob says, raising an eyebrow at Rachel and Cody's make out session. Grimacing at the scene, I turn feeling repulsed thinking about the other lips Cody has touched.

"Yes, it happens a lot. " I admit getting a booming laugh from Jacob which catches me off guard.

"You don't seem happy about it."

"Why should I?" I respond by lifting my shoulder stubbornly. "Whenever Cody is around, Sarah and I become invisible. The only person who can break through to Rachel in that state is Jordan maybe".

"Who is Jordan?" asks Jacob, looking at Rachel differently. "Does she have another man and do they both know about each other?"

At that, I can't help but giggle. Rachel has never been unfaithful and certainly never with Jordan.

"Jordan is Rachel's seven-year-old brother and the most precious thing in her life." I reveal finally as Jacob nods, understanding why it's funny.

"He must be a special boy".

"Yes, he is," I laugh, meaning every word because Jordan is one unique child indeed. Jordan is an earth wizard a male version of a witch.

Jordan's gifts manifested over the last couple of years. Rachel, the overprotective sister she is, is trying to keep it a secret. Wizards for some reason in the western region of Perta, are treated like freaks for having magic.

Some men feel like magic is a woman's domain. It is correct that a woman is more likely of the sexes to get a magical gift, but men can inherit it too.

And that is Jordan's case, and Rachel refuses to let anyone abuse him because of it. And who could blame her, Rachel has raised him since Gail, their mother only cares about her oldest sons.

Shaking my head, I try not to think about Rachel's home life and get back to my current problem. Sarah and Mark are getting a little too close in my opinion as I gaze at the two individuals flirting with each other.. Okay time to break up this love fest I thought.

"We should get going before it gets too late," stating to Jacob. The green-eyed royal is about to reply but I already left heading to Mark and Sarah.

"Your Highness, we should be departing soon, my father goes to bed early." I interrupt the two with a fib knowing my father is a night owl.

Sarah gives me a look at that statement but chooses not to unravel my lie . "Yes, Andy's right, you should get going. " She says, making her exit and I almost did a happy dance. The plan is successful. Sarah and the prince will be separated but my hopes are destroyed in seconds.

"Wait" Prince Mark shouts, grabbing Sarah's hand stopping her departure. "Can't you come along with us." At that moment, I am sure Sarah would have swooned if she could.

"I don't want to impose on the Miller family" she squeaks out.

Shaking his head Mark looks defiant, and I get a feeling he isn't used to being rejected. "I'm sure the Millers can take one more guest right Andy?" The prince asks and the focus turns back to me. Biting back a curse I want to disagree but cannot.

"Yes, come Sarah, we have plenty of room." I say in a fake cheerful voice. Luckily Mark is distracted rambling to Sarah to notice. Frowning, I want to pull my hair out at how things are turning out. It's only a matter of time before Sarah reveals she is a water witch. And once that happens I'll be waving my goodbyes to her because Mark will propose. In that case that information can never be divulged, making me grin. Maybe all is not lost although I might need some assistance in the matter as I go gather Rachel.

Jacob

My normally peaceful walk home is not what I call tranquil. Ten soldiers march alongside me making grunting noises. Plus the ramblings of Mark and Sarah are driving me slowly insane. They are practically lovebirds and Sarah just had to demonstrate her magic. With a lift of her hand water flows out of her canteen and forms a ball. Mark claps at her performance and Sarah smiles in appreciation..

Looking at them you would not think they just met only moments ago. I scowl in annoyance that my plan of keeping the two apart is ruined.

"That death stare is not helping anything Andy "Rachel mumbles beside me. Turning to her I try to hide my tense expression but fail.

"Sarah is practically begging to be taken away. Why are you not worried?"

"If it's love why should I interfere "Rachel says looking envious at Mark and Sarah. "I wish Cody was like that sometimes instead of just the physical stuff."

"Maybe you should tell him that instead of me." I declare not interested in my friend's problems with Cody.

"Don't get me wrong. I do like the feeling of him being close to me and his warmth. And when he touches me my mind goes to mush." Rachel babbles going into too much detail for my innocent ears.

"No, no, no." I refuse to hear anymore sordid details. Frowning at me Rachel reaches for my hands struggling to move them.

"Andy, listen to me!!!"

" No, I will not let my innocent ears be corrupted." I scream which ends with Rachel and myself on the ground trying to pin each other.

My taller friend had the advantage of longer limbs, but I'm stronger. Easily pushing the other girl off me.

Cold water appears before us splashing our faces. We both glare at the reason why standing before us.

"Girls, we are not children anymore, act like adults" Sarah lectures, spraying more water on us. "Cool down and grow up." At that moment our sweet friend turns into our mothers before our eyes. I laugh thinking of the comparison as Rachel takes revenge.

Taking a handful of wet earth she flings it at Sarah's face hitting the brown haired girl. A big hunk of mud slid off her angry face and the fight is on with water and mud flying in the air. Not wanting to be left out I prepare my own mud balls when a loud whistling sound cuts off our battle.

Standing in the middle of our fight is Mark and Jacob with very amused expressions. "As much as I enjoy mud and water being thrown everywhere. I think we should get going ladies." Mark interjects by handing a cloth to Sarah to wipe her face.

"Sorry Mark, this is just how we settle our problems." Sarah giggles wiping the mud from her face.

"We've been doing this since we were children and I'm still undefeated." Rachel announces raising her hands like a champion boxer.

"Lies" Sarah and I argue together!!

"Fine ladies, we will have a rematch later" Rachel promises. "Get ready to lose."

"Okay, same wagers" Sarah proposes, her face bright with excitement.

"Losers do the winner's chores for a day." Rachel lays out the rules and with both of us nodding she grabs our wrists. "Okay the wager is agreed, and the promise of friends declared."Saying the chant together twice then spinning around, all three of us spit on the ground to seal the arrangement.

"You girls are weird," Jacob says, watching us like we're a new species of animal. Blushing Sarah hides her face in her hands, but Rachel stands proudly.

"We are not weird, but unique," she states, making everyone laugh. "Now let's get back to business and get these royals to Mr. Miller's house." With that Rachel goes to the front of our line and begins leading the way.

"She's very" Mark ponders to find the word for it. "Assertive. " Sarah and I share a look and chuckle." I don't mean anything rude by it but honestly she's very strong minded." He explains rubbing his neck looking so mortified that I give him a reprieve.

"Rachel is the middle child of four brothers so being pushy is a way of life for her." I respond looking at Rachel pointing out sights to the enamored soldiers beside her.

"Well, we need more Rachel's where I come from." Jacob declares next to me looking at her with admiration. "Someone who isn't afraid to face down a large crowd of people to come to a friend's defense is my kind of girl".

Smiling at that comment. I can't agree more.

"Speaking of the incident, what happened back there Andy "Sarah asks. "It usually takes more for you to lose control and I didn't even see Matthew there."

"I don't want to talk about it." I answer in a groan.

Pressing her lips together Sarah gives me a stern gaze. "Andy the truth, or I will get Rachel over here. And you know she will force you to speak even if she has to hold you down".

Shivering at the threat knowing how accurate it would be. Relenting, I start my tale at meeting the princes. After that I spoke of how Tim Walker pushed me and ended with the marriage that Cody brought up.

"Marriage, you are getting married?" Sarah shrieks.

"No, it is false. My father wouldn't discuss something like that without me.

"Sometimes fathers do things behind their children's backs they don't know." Sarah utters, getting a faraway look in her eyes. I know she is thinking about what happened a year ago. Her father John tried to sell her to a local man to settle his debts. Robert Smith was a crook in every way and was no decent pick for anyone's sixteen-year-old daughter, but John didn't care.

He only cared about settling his debts. Fortunately, my father ran Robert out of town before Sarah was forced to marry him.

"Well, my father is an honest man who takes my opinion into consideration" I object.

"I know that Andy. Your father would never do anything like that ." Sarah says quickly realizing what she said might be an insult. "And besides you two are practically one and the same".

Rolling my eyes at what she says I move away from her previous statement. "Of course, Father always said I am his double and we could finish each other's sentences. I am lucky I am not a boy, or he would have called me Junior instead of Andy".

"Well with that mouth of yours I can hardly tell" Sarah jokes with me as I playfully lunge for her. She evades me and runs to catch up with Rachel. Rachel is so focused on leading the soldiers, she shrieks when Sarah appears behind her making the horses whine. Seeing the laughter on everyone's face Rachel is not in the least bit embarrassed. She only curtsy and pulls a giggling Sarah along with her.

Shaking my head at my friends' behavior, I nearly miss what Mark says. " Andy is Sarah engaged or spoken for. "

"What?" I stumbled out trying to confirm what I just heard.

Mark asks again. "Do you know if Sarah is promised to another or is courting someone now?" I know if I lie about Sarah's relationship it might get Mark to pursue another woman. However if the truth is found out it could mean dire consequences to Weston. And right now, the village's needs outweigh my own selfish ones.

"No one is courting Sarah, and she has no marriage contract." I answer grimly which gets Jacob's attention, but Mark looks like he is floating right now. His pale face lit up as he straightened his posture.

"Well that is great news for me" he says with a smile. "My plan of seeing if we are compatible will not be interrupted. Excuse me, I think it is time for me to get to know my future wife." And with that Mark left us to reunite with Sarah.

"He can't be serious?"

"Oh, he is. Mark takes everything seriously," Jacob answers.

"How could he say that they just met?" I argue flinging my hands in the air over the prince's foolishness. "Marriage is serious and shouldn't be rushed into suddenly."

"In our case, it is different since we have to find a bride in a short time. Maybe love comes more naturally to some, and it only takes one glance to find your perfect match." When he says these words something in my belly flips, but I ignored it? Sarah is my top priority, not some funny feeling in the pit of my stomach.

"Well, it shouldn't be", I announce. If what you're saying is factual Matthew Walker and I should be lovebirds at this moment.

Giving me an intense look, Jacob seems more attentive. "This man, does he fancy you?" The way his voice deepens makes me quiver inside that it spooks me. Trying to forget the strange feeling, I think of Matthew, and that certainly put a damper on things.

"Yes, he has been trying to court me since I turned fifteen two years ago.It doesn't matter how many times I refuse him, he still won't accept that I don't like him."

"Is he handsome?" Jacob inquires.

Shrugging I respond "Matthew is good-looking, but his attitude towards people makes me disagree with him."

"Explain it to me."

"He's a bully, something I can't overlook."

At my answer Jacob smiles. "I agree with that statement because it doesn't matter how beautiful a person is. If their personality doesn't match their appearance the person might as well be ugly."

"You are correct there, and I cannot take another rude blond in my life." I confess thinking of Mel and Ella.

"Who is the other rude blond in your life?" Jacob asks.

I hesitate for a minute, deciding whether I should tell him the truth or a load of crap. I determine the truth would be a better option, since he will be meeting Mel and Ella soon.

"My sister and mother are quite a duo to deal with." I finally admit trying to be careful with my approach. Yet Jacob knows I am holding something back.

"How so?" He prods trying to get me to clarify more.

"They act like they are superior to everyone just because of their looks and magic. To them, having these abilities makes them better than others, especially me." I divulge feeling my face get hotter hating talking about my weaknesses in front of people.

"What magic do you have?" Jacob asks with no judgment in his voice. It surprised me but I know the remarks are coming soon about my useless gift.

"I am a Seer." I reveal, waiting for the negative remarks but none never come. When I look at Jacob, I see amazement and shock.

"That's wonderful. You can see the future, why are you not happier about it."

"It's just that my magic hasn't been all that great." I shrug. "My grandmother Ruth has the gift too. Her magic shows dangers but mine only predicts births or trivial things. Unfortunately, foresight isn't grand like elemental magic and not useful in the fields." I take a breath looking at Jacob wanting him to understand. "My gift doesn't do anything for the village, and it's considered pointless next to others."

"Perhaps it takes time for magic to grow. That can explain why your grandmother's magic is stronger than yours. I think your gift will shine in the future and you shouldn't rush it.. And try not to be hard on yourself, it's damaging to your self-confidence."

Going over his words, I can see the logic in them. Always disappointed about what my magic can't do; I'm not appreciating what it can accomplish. Maybe what grandmother Ruth said is right, I will see places and people in time. I just need to be patient.

"Thanks, that helps a little bit." I say honestly and with that Jacob gives me a smirk that I want to wipe off. "However, you're kind of a jerk at times." Commenting not caring about his noble status.

"Oh, so I am a jerk so I guess I can do this." He quips reaching around my waist and lifting me up in the air.

"Put me down." I squeal though it quickly transforms into a giggle when he twirls me around in the air.

"Not until you apologize for the jerk comment. " Jacob refuses, twirling me even faster.

Trying to frown yet it is impossible as more giggles come out. "Okay you aren't a jerk now put me down, before I lose my lunch.

"I wouldn't want a lady to become sick." Jacob declares, putting me on the ground. It takes me a minute to get my bearing back, and I realize his hands are still around my waist. Feeling eyes on me, I can see Mark and my friends with identical grins watching us.

Embarrassed, I remove his hands and give my smirking friends a glare. "Why did no one come to my rescue?"

Rachel and Sarah glance at each other before answering.

"We didn't think you wanted our help Andy," Rachel says with a grin.

"And we didn't want to interrupt your new romance" Sarah adds with a giggle.

I'm stunned at the outrageous comments that I'm waiting for Jacob to refute. Instead all I get is his smirk growing more prominent. "Why are you not saying anything? My friends just accused us of flirting with each other."

At that all I get in response is Jacob waving happily at my traitor friends. "Thank you ladies, for being so lovely and next time we'll do it in private" he yells out.

My mouth is open and my friends are nearly on the ground in glee. "Okay my prince now we know to separate you from Andy." Rachel says in a severe tone which only lasts a minute before a laugh comes out. Rolling my eyes, I know she is having the time of her life at my expense.

"Get the giggles out but as soon as Cody sticks his tongue down your throat. Payback is coming my friend." I vow to Rachel who isn't the least bit concerned.

"I enjoy Cody's tongue any day of the week." She announces then adds slyly. "Although I'm sure Jacob's tongue will be keeping you busy soon also." My friend winks making Mark laugh along with a few of the soldiers too.

"Fine, have your fun" I grumble, submitting to the teasing moving to the front of the line. There I realize we are standing on top of the hill to my house. In the distance I can see the red cobblestone and a woman's figure glaring down at us.

Seeing the apron and the mature body, I know it is Ella. Probably waiting to scream at me for being late for dinner. "Well let's get this over with" I mumble marching up the last couple of feet to my home. I must look like a sight, plain Andy Miller, leading a group of armed men to my house to meet my parents. I want to yell out I'm the pied piper of men but I'm sure Ella would say something negative about it.

Finally I reach the house and Ella doesn't wait to scold me. "How dare you be late" she yells. "We had to hold dinner because your father was worried that you got hurt. Instead all you were doing was gallivanting around with your disgusting friends". Pointing at Rachel in particular when she says the insult.

"A pleasure seeing you too Mrs.Miller." Rachel responds back earning a glare from Ella.

"Rachel, still with that sharp tongue of yours. No wonder Cody hasn't asked you to marry him yet." My mother taunts knowing it's a sore subject for Rachel.. "Andy, your friend is as much of a disappointment as you. Send her away, I don't want two future old maids in my house" she orders .

"No, I'm not doing that. Rachel is my friend and is welcome here anytime she pleases." I refuse my mother's request instantly, I'm tired of her rudeness to my friends especially Rachel. Ella hates my friend because she is stronger than Mel and everyone knows it. She believe Rachel is taking my sister's spotlight making her the enemy in her mind

Angry at my refusal, Ella grabs me by the ear before I can react. "Don't speak to me that way. The sight of you disgusts me to my core and you have the nerve to argue with me. You're late and ruining my night for your disrespectful friends."Her rant wouldn't have been so bad. If we didn't have an audience of strangers witnessing the whole debacle.

"Mother I can explain but you need to listen." I warn trying to get her attention on our guests.

"I don't care about your excuses," screams Ella, shaking my arm." I cannot believe I have a horrible daughter like you."

"Mrs. Miller, get your hands off your daughter and let her explain" Jacob demands losing his temper. His voice dumbfounds Ella and my hand is released. Ella can only stare at Jacob and the other armed men wearing displeased expressions on their faces..

Pulling a smile on her face Ella tries to remedy the situation." My apologies, I didn't see you there." These words didn't lessen the frowns she's receiving from her previous statements.

"Of course, you didn't see us because you were berating Andy for no good reason." Jacob replies and I feel better hearing him stand up for me.

"I was wrong to assume the worst about my daughter." Ella concedes quickly to the royals but not to me. I decide to let it go and move on before a disagreement starts.

"Mother let me introduce you to Jacob of Polla." I announce pointing to Jacob who continues to scowl at Ella. " And Prince Mark of Gallopia" I gesture to Mark next.

Her mouth slides open in awe as she stutters. "Your Highnesses, what brings you to my humble home?"

"They're here to see Father," I explained quickly. "Can you go retrieve him for them?"

"Certainly," Ella answers motherly towards me, but her eyes are cold. The message is clear: she's faking being kind to me for appearances. Turning around she rushes into the house like it is on fire.

I let out a sigh when she is gone." Is your mother always this unpleasant to you?" Jacob asks with some rage in his voice.

"This is as good as it gets," I confirm honestly.

"You're right. The blonds in your life are nightmares." Jacob agrees, making me smile before the door reopens. Coming out the door father makes his entrance with Ella close behind.

"Andy, I hear you brought me some visitors." Father says giving me a big hug. Something about my father's presence made things less tense with everyone. Jacob calms down and the soldiers stop glowering at Ella.

"Yes, father, I brought you some royals who want to speak about the crops." I inform him after that Jacob and Mark introduce themselves. In a matter of minutes, my father has both men in a fit of laughter.

"Rachel and Sarah, how are you girls doing?" My father greets both girls with a hug.

"Tired but good Mr. Miller." Rachel remarks for Sarah and herself.

"Hopefully not too tired to join us for dinner." Father proposes giving both girls an invitation to dinner.

"Andrew, the girls might have dinner plans. Besides, the royals would not want extra guests at the table" Ella argues.

"We already asked them to join us, Madam. So please do not presume what we want." Mark refutes in a scornful voice next to Sarah.

Realizing the folly, Ella tries to mend matters. "My mistake, please come in and have some tea." She offers morphing into a hostess while opening the door to our home.

"We should tend to our horses first. Can we use your barn and supplies." Jacob requests and when I am about to answer, Ella's voice beats me to it.

"Of course, we have plenty of supplies," she says. Turning to me, Ella furnished a stern stare. "Andy, go take the prince's men to the barn and help tend to their horses."

Nodding, I move to leave to escort the soldiers to our barn. " I will come along also to make sure my horses are being cared for properly" Jacob volunteers.

" Your Highness, Andy can handle this mundane task." Ella states wrapping her arms around Jacob's bicep. "Come meet my eldest daughter Melissa, I think you and her will hit it off brilliantly." She hints and I can see her already scheming trying to get a royal for my sister.

She pulls Jacob towards the house until he removes her hands from his body. "I'd rather help with the horses than to talk idly." He says quickly, grabbing my hand and pulling me to the barn. Yelling after us, Ella looks ready to faint at the notion a prince didn't want to meet Mel.

"I think you just shattered my mother's mind."

"I cannot say I'm unapologetic about it. If your sister is similar to your mother, the barn is a blessing. " He conveys and I can understand his feelings, especially knowing my family. I show Jacob and his men the barn which isn't really big. Ten stalls is all that the barn can fit and only one houses a horse. We keep the others free in case of guests and the supplies are located not too far from the stalls. Food is quickly laid out and the horses require a good brushing. I decided to assist in that task grooming a handsome black stallion. The beast has a remarkable black coat that is dingy which I will happily fix.

" I am going to make you look beautiful." I coo at the horse kissing his nose.

"Stop talking to Storm like a baby. He's a battle horse" Jacob points out.

Ignoring him, I continue talking in that manner to Storm. Storm seems to respond to me listening to every word I am saying. "He seems to like my voice. I think he might like me better than you."

"Or you might remind him of the red-haired mare he fancies." Jacob alleges barely dodging the carrot I throw at him.

"Hey, that's very rude. To think I was going to thank you for defending me to my mother earlier." I mutter turning my back playfully knowing his comments weren't malicious. " Anyway about that, why did you come to my aid with my mother?"

"Why would I not?" Jacob simply says. "I cannot watch someone being demeaned in my presence and not help."

Feeling the tears come to my eyes I hold them in. What Jacob said touched me? "Well, I appreciate it. Not many people would do that for a stranger."

"Where I grew up, someone picking on another is frowned upon? And that's what your mother was doing." He says with so much force I believe him. After that we drop into silence until I notice someone is missing.

"Jacob, where is Mark?" I ask, trying to remember what happened to the other royal.

"He went inside to try to win Sarah's heart," Jacob chuckles at his remark. " He really adores your friend Andy, it's almost fun watching him make a fool out of himself while flirting. "

" He's still going on with that nonsense. " I roar thinking of the prince and wondering if he's a scoundrel." Does he flirt with every girl he sees." I question hoping for a positive answer. If Mark is just a flirt I have nothing to worry about.

Jacob eyes me suspiciously before replying. " I've known Mark for a long time. That's not in his character. If he is going after Sarah then she's the one for him."

Letting go of the brush in my hand I can't allow Mark to get any closer to Sarah. I'm about to march out of the barn when a hand grabs me. "Let go of me" I bark at Jacob, the person restraining me.

" I know what you're about to do Andy,and I cannot allow it. Mark has every right to claim Sarah under the rules of the festival." Jacob argues using those stupid laws of the Princess Festival against me.

I try to twist out of his grip to stop Mark from stealing Sarah away. Angrily pulling and scratching but nothing helps. "Why should I stand by and let a stranger take my best friend?" I scream hitting Jacob in the chest in front of the soldiers.

They are one step away from interfering although Jacob stops them with a command. " Halt leave us for a moment. " And with that order the men disperse.

Drawing me closer, he brings me into a hug securing my hands to my side. All I can do now is fall apart in his arms. "It's not fair, he cannot take her, she is ours, not his" I wail!

"Maybe she is meant to be his now". He says softly rubbing my hair. His words stick in my mind as whiteness overcomes my vision. I know what is happening. My foresight is activating and it can't be a worse time.

Pushing away from Jacob I find a stall to lean against before my body freezes. Images flash into my head all at once overwhelming my brain. My foresight sometimes shows little parts first like a baby being born before it gets to the main event. It's kind of annoying especially since the gift restricts your body until it finishes showing you the vision.

Something must have been said to activate my magic. Looking through the images in my mind one is coming to me clearly. Drawing myself into the vision, I am amazed by what I'm seeing. A majestic white church with ancient writing on the bricks that I cannot understand. Looking around I see people arriving at the church dressed fancy.

Concentrating, I willed myself inside the church. Inside I find hundreds of people all watching the center of the room. Going over to see what the fuss is about I see flowers and linens draped everywhere. The place is beautifully decorated but that isn't the most stunning thing in the room. A woman wearing a white lace dress that curves around her body like a glove. The lace veil falls over her face and her straight brown hair is curled tightly at the end. The makeup is understated with just red lipstick to make her mouth pop. It's heartbreaking taking her in because this person is someone I know well. I recognize another person in the room standing next to a priest.

Mark appears clean shaven and his hair trim wearing a crown on top of his head. The prince proudly gazes at Sarah walking towards him. Sarah seems to share the same emotion when she reaches Mark at the center of the church. It hurts me to realize I am seeing their wedding and that means Sarah will leave us soon.

I feel resigned and angry at the same time. Why did my magic have to work this time and show me this? I could have lived without knowing that in the future Sarah will be gone from my life forever. My mood breaks my concentration and the vision slips away forcing me back into my body.

Feeling shaky, my eyesight is a little blurry due to my magic. My bearing returns to me and Jacob is in front of me with guards surrounding us. Seeing my eyes open Jacob blows a sigh of relief and screams out an order. "Go get her some water."

Before anyone can go I speak up. "Please don't leave, it's normal. " Jacob is about to argue with me when I straighten up looking completely healthy. His green eyes analyze my every movement in awe at my recovery. "I am fine gentlemen, just one of the perks of being a Seer."

The soldiers accept my explanation and get back to work. Yet Jacob seems less sure, scanning me carefully. " I never seen anything like that before, it looked like you fainted."

"Yes, it can be surprising when you first see it." I agree impatiently not wanting to talk right now." We should get back to work." Grabbing a brush, I move to groom another horse.

"What did you see?" Jacob beckoning clearly not understanding my attempts to avoid the conversation.

"It was nothing." I choke out trying to block out Sarah's wedding from my mind..

"It's something, so tell me" he demands.

"You aren't my father so don't tell me what to do." I screech, throwing my brush across the barn before fleeing. I have to get away from his questioning and process this new information my magic showed me. Information that will come true because my foresight is never wrong. The future or fate is what my grandmother calls it is unstoppable and only fools try to avoid it.

Ignoring the tears that begin to fall I pause for a second. Closing my eyes I focus on the sound of the wind. It calms me enough to notice the heavy footsteps coming my way. Swinging around I see Jacob running towards me only stopping when we are steps away from each other.

Breathing harshly his eyes are sharp taking in my tear stained face. Sighing he hands me a cloth to wipe my face. "I want an explanation but ,obviously this isn't the right time."

"Thanks, and sorry for what I said in the barn." I apologize feeling a little ashamed for taking my frustration out on him.

"It's forgotten so let's go inside and see what our friends are doing." Jacob says, giving me his arm to take. A slow grin takes shape on my face as I place my hand on his arm. I let myself be led in and try to focus on the present. The future isn't in my control and worrying about it isn't productive at all right now. If Sarah is destined to leave she will go sooner or later. For now I should enjoy what is left of my time with her.

51

Tollar Stone

Walking into the house on the arm of Jacob I feel a little awkward. However, the familiar sound of my father's voice gives me enough courage to continue on. Our friends and my father are all in the sitting room having some tea. Father is the first to notice our arrival with a sly glance.

Trying to figure out why I realize my hand is still on Jacob's arm. Blushing, I drop his hand and move several steps away.

Jacob just shrugs off my reaction going over to sit next to Mark. Who to my displeasure is right next to Sarah chatting. Frowning at that, I almost didn't hear my father's voice. "Andy, don't stand there like a tree. Come sit down next to your dear old dad."

"Father, you aren't old." I comment on taking the spot next to him.

"Yes, I am and soon you'll be taking care of me."

"Fine, when that day comes I will hire a maid to take care of you."

"Oh you will hire a maid. What kind of cold-hearted daughter did I raise?"

"One who will not bat an eye if you fall on your face." I counter earning a laugh from father and the royals. Feeling like my old self again, I let myself be dragged into a conversation with Rachel until Mel makes her entrance.

Walking down the stairs Mel has on a blue dress that shows off her breasts and makes her waist tinier. Her hair is curled and her white skin glows, yet her appearance did not impress the royals.. Both men aren't gawking at my sister which seems to frustrate her.

"Hello your Highnesses, I'm Melissa Miller, a witch of the earth." Mel says using the introduction mother taught us for the royals. People believe if a royal knows what type of witch a woman is it improves her chances.

"Nice to meet you Melissa, I am Prince Mark of Gallopia and this is Jacob of Polla." At hearing his title I can imagine my sister plotting her next move. Scanning the area around the royals she notices the spots are taken by my friends.

Huffing Mel has no choice but to sit next to father and myself. She sends lethal glares towards Rachel and Sarah, probably thinking they are after the princes themselves. And sadly in Mel's warp mind, that makes them the enemy.. Shaking my head at the thought, I overheard father telling the royals of Weston's problems.

"I'll explain why there's a decline in our crops for your nations. Our fields have been getting attacked by Delianians for a year now. We lost many crops and good people because of it. The money we have now isn't enough to hire a militia. I'm afraid Weston, if things do not change, will be gone soon."

Father's words grips everyone in shock and horror. The only person not bothered is Mel who is batting her eyes at Jacob. To his credit looks just as upset at the news as I do.

"We thought it was a drought, not the Delianians attacking Perta too." He says dropping a huge piece of information in our lap.

" They are causing trouble in Polla too." I am completely stunned at this new information.

"For a year now our Elite Archers are holding them at bay. "Jacob says with most of us amaze at hearing about the legendary group that skills and accuracy protects Polla.

"It's not just Polla, my kingdom is having similar problems." Mark confirms giving us worried looks. "I don't know what the Delianians are planning, but we need to find out."

"I agree, it's lucky you chose to come to Weston for the festival" Rachel responds.

"We did not really have a choice. The stone directed us that we will find our brides here" Mark replies confusing me.

" What do you mean by "directed us"? It seems a little off that someone had to tell you to come here to our Princess Festival?" Both Mark and Jacob give me anxious looks. "Say something" I yell, making Mark speak up.

"Andy, have you ever wondered why there are not more Princess Festivals? Only twelve are held in twenty different nations so it cannot be random. Our ancestors are the reason for this way of organizing the Festival. They made a way for their descendants to find their brides without constantly searching."

" What did your ancestors do" questions Sarah?

"They summoned the most powerful witches at the time to help them." Jacob told us like he was a storyteller. "They wanted them to figure out a way for them to find a bride easier. It took two years for ten witches to accomplish this method but it had a cost. The witches found a stone that could absorb magic and the wisest of them placed her magic inside of it. The stone only worked when she sacrificed her power so it could predict our soulmates locations."

"What was the magic that powered the stone?" Rachel curiously asks.

"Foresight" Jacob claims, surprising me.

"You're lying, " Rachel accuses. " No witch would voluntarily lose her power.." She says out loud what we're all thinking. A witch is linked to her magic, it's part of her nature. To freely give that up is like cutting off a healthy leg.

"We aren't lying. The witch that gave up her magic was named Tollar. The stone now carries the same name as her" Mark argues.

"Very funny we aren't simpletons" I contend.

"Andy, it's true the Tollar Stone exists" my father says supporting the royals claims. My mouth drops. How is this true?

" How do you know Mr. Miller" Sarah probes for more information.

"I'm the village leader of Weston. I get notified when the stone tells if the bride's location is here. The secret has been handed down from generation to generation." Father clarifying the procedure of the Princess Festival in detail.

"You're really letting a stone pick your spouses." Rachel asks, directing the question to the royals in disbelief.

"Our parents are in happy marriages, why not" replies Mark.

"Do you see a vision of your bride with the stone?" I wonder if it's like my own foresight.

"No, we just get their personality, magic and their location. That's why the festival is important to gather the necessary people."

"In that case, why have we not heard of it?" Rachel declares.

"Our ancestors wisely thought telling potential brides they were chosen because of a magical stone wasn't a good idea." Jacob explains in a no nonsense way making Rachel laugh.

After that, our conversations go back to the safer topics. "Andy, we have to get up bright and early to settle the budget for the festival." Father reminds me of the planning that goes with this big event.

"I'll remember, have you confirmed if the Sinclair's are doing the dart booth. " I question trying to verify the things we need to do.

"Not yet, we will ask tomorrow." Seeing my face drop, father tries to be positive. "My twin, do not worry we can handle this." I groan at the speech thinking of the long days of work awaiting us.

"I guess no rest for the gingers" Rachel comments seeing my misery.

"If they convince Mrs. Moore to sell her blueberry pie at the festival. Then Andy sacrificing sleep is worth it" Sarah squeals, licking her lips.

"Getting Mrs. Moore to sell her cookies was hard enough. The pies might be impossible" I announce ignoring their protest and whines.

" Come on Andy! Use that stubbornness of yours to get us pies." Rachel demands getting a glare back from me.

"That woman gave me the evil eye for asking her to switch locations with Mr. Charles's lemonade stand." I yell remembering the quarrel I had with the baker. For a woman in her early thirties, Mrs. Moore is pickier than any grandmother can be.

"Your neighbors seem to be a lively bunch" Mark laughs at my outburst.

"They are lovely until you cross them and get banned from eating their delicious pie." I gripe earning amusement at my expense. "Not funny. I cannot have that sweet goodness in my mouth until Mrs. Moore forgives me." Only receiving more laughter at my misfortune.

"It's decided I have to try this pie now" Jacob proclaims.

"Don't ruin your palate, it's nothing special." Mel criticizes earning an eye roll from me. She always gets snarky when someone else is praised, not her.

"I think her pies are wonderful" Sarah comments, earning a glare from my sister.

" It is not surprising that you'll speak on the issue.Nonetheless I cannot say you are a good judge Sarah. You will eat *anything* put in front of your fat face." At that remark Mel cruelly laughs making Sarah cry.

"Melissa, apologize now!!" Father orders.

"Why Sarah is fat I'm just stating a fact. Besides, the royals shouldn't waste their time on undesirable people." Mel rants gesturing at Sarah in particular. "Weston is filled with them including Mrs. Moore the pie lady everyone adores. She is still the woman who could not keep a roof over her head and had to be taken in by family."

"Her husband died and she landed on tough times. That has nothing to do with her character" Rachel argues.

"Yes, it does and I'm certain the royals will agree with me." Mel cackling, missing the angry glares thrown her way by the nobles..

Feeling angry and ashamed I'm about to speak up but someone beat me to it.

"Everyone rich or poor has value to their existence, don't you agree Jacob." Mark asks, looking at his friend trying to compose himself.

"Yes I agree, our mothers were once what Melissa called undesirable." Jacob declares his green eyes sharpen taking in Mel's shocked face

"Our mothers were poorer than dirt before they met our fathers. They taught us the kindness and the harshness of people's souls which is their true value. And right now, yours is telling us a lot about you Melissa" Mark answers coldly.

"Your Highness, I didn't know about your mothers" my sister whimpers.

"There is still no excuse to speak that way. And I want you to get rid of that disillusioned idea of making one of us your husband." Mark commands harshly, shattering Mel's dreams. " Our soulmates are not hateful people and you are one of the people that we despise the most.."

Tearfully Mel glances at the royals after the speech." I'm sorry" she cries, fleeing the room in a hurry.After that humiliation I will be awed if Mel even shows up for dinner tonight. The scolding was well deserved, especially at how my sister was speaking about Sarah and Mrs Moore. It was about time someone reprimanded Mel and I'm glad it was the royals.

Silence follows as everyone digests what happened moments ago. Honestly I don't know what was worse. Mel making a fool out of herself or the aftermath. A throat clearing brings everyone's eyes to my father. "I am deeply sorry about my eldest daughter. I did not teach that behavior and certainly don't condone it."

"We don't blame you Andrew. Melissa has her own mind and beliefs." Mark states firmly leaving no room for disagreement. I'm actually happy when Ella walks in the room giving everyone a gleaming smile breaking the tension.

"Can I get anyone something to drink?" She asks but the question is directed to the royals not the other occupants. Everyone picks up on the slight quickly and the atmosphere is very hostile.

"No, we're fine," Mark says too harshly, catching Ella's attention. She is about to say something else but father interferes.

"Dinner smells good, we should all go to the dining area. "He motions everyone to follow him to the next room. The only thing in the room is our cedar table that seats ten in the center. Once everyone is inside, father points to the kitchen." Girls, come help me with the food." And with that Rachel, Sarah and I go with him to the kitchen. In the room a turkey and many side dishes were scattered around us. Reaching for one of the dishes, father stops me. "Don't bring in anything right now; I need to talk to you girls."

"What is it, Mr. Miller?" Rachel asks, leaning against the wall.

"Girls, you know the issues facing our village and without a wealthy ally Weston is gone." Father explains looking a little worried.

"We know that father, that's why we are going to ask for money at the Princess Festival." I answer, not understanding his worry.

"Andy, I don't think that will be enough anymore." He mumbles, rubbing a withered hand over his face.

"Mr. Miller, we cannot give up on Weston" Rachel says encouragingly." There's got to be a way of getting what we need from the princes."

"How, you heard of their problems with the Delianians." Sarah points out. " Helping us against them will cause them more issues. Our village's crops were our currency and that's no more why, will they aid us."

Sarah's statement hit me hard because it's true. Our crops were our only leverage which we do not have anymore. I never thought of the possibility that the royals might abandon us.

"I have an idea, but some of you might not like it." Father says slowly, looking at all of our faces with concern.

"Dad, what do you need of us." I demand refusing to give up.

"The Princes have to be connected to Weston on a personal level. The best way of doing that is with a marriage and I believe two of you can accomplish that. "

"What!!" Rachel and Sarah shouts in surprise but I'm able to hold mine in. Thinking of my vision in the barn is *Sarah's marriage the key to saving Weston. If that's the case maybe this was not a bad thing after all.*

Father gestures for us to focus because he has more to say. "I think both Princes might pick one of you girls by my observations I saw earlier." Father declares, giving us all sad looks. "I know what I am asking you is unfair. Yet I can't see another way out of this mess".

"Mr. Miller, I'm already in a relationship." Rachel argues looking disturbed at even being asked.

"I know Rachel, this is more about Andy and Sarah." Father replies making Rachel calmer but now I'm panicking.

"Me. You want me to marry a stranger?" I choke out. How can my father ask me to marry a total stranger who is a prince. He is nuts. I'm the total opposite of what these men wanted. " Dad, no royal would marry me in a million years." I protest looking at Rachel for support but she agrees with father.

" Andy, Jacob does seem enamored with you. He even held your hand without prodding" she says making me blush.

"He was just being a gentleman," I state quickly. " And let's be serious men like Jacob go for great beauties like Mel, not me." I huff blowing a loose curl out of my face. "I am not powerful and any royal with half a brain would not choose trash like me." It hurts saying it aloud, but it's the truth.

I feel tears roll down my face and a giant hand wipes them away. "That's not true, any man royal or commoner will be lucky to call you their wife." Father says gently hugging me. "I should have stopped your mother from saying those things to you." I am about to argue, but Father shakes his head. "It's true, because right now you cannot even see your worthiness. Andy, all today you had Jacob charmed and was not aware of it."

"That's impossible, he was just being nice." I murmur, not quite believing what I'm hearing.

"Oh it's true!" replies Rachel with a smile on her face. "He's been watching and speaking to you since both of you met.".

"He was teasing me Rachel" I maintain.

"My daughter, a man, only teases the girl he likes." Father answers for Rachel, shutting me up for good. Can it be possible all this time Jacob liked me. "Now that Andy's doubts are gone, what do you girls say?" He continues not waiting for my mind to process this information." Will you marry the royals for the good of Weston?"

Thinking about this, everything in me wants to say no. I didn't want to be trapped with a stranger for the rest of my life like my parents. Watching their marriage showed me the type of union I did not desire.

"I'll do it," Sarah announces, her face glowing red. "I cannot promise you I will get chosen but I'll do my best for Weston." Her meek response catches us all off guard. Looking at her, I can see she had her doubts but is still willing to do her part.. She inspires me to do the same in that instant.

"Okay, if Jacob loses his marbles and chooses me. I will get him to help Weston" I pledge earning a grin from father and Rachel.

" I'm glad that everything is settled.Now, let's feed these hungry people, girls." He declares grabbing the turkey and leaving us alone in the kitchen. I stare at Sarah trembling in place looking at the door. Neither of us move towards the door out of nervousness. It's laughable that Weston's future is in the hands of a shy girl and a tomboy.

"Go on ladies, your future suitors await you." Rachel laughs placing dishes into mine and Sarah's hands forcing us out of the door.

A Better Life

Stumbling out the kitchen door, I barely caught myself and the food. Sarah isn't so fortunate slipping and only being saved by Mark grabbing her around the waist. Although he cannot balance the food dishes and they waste on his shirt. Sarah looks mortified for her part and tries to apologize, but Mark dismisses it.

"Don't worry it was an accident." He says escorting a stun Sarah to the table where the others are waiting.

"That worked better than I planned." Rachel gloats behind me.

I send a glare at the tall girl, not liking her scheme at all. "You could have made Sarah and I fall down. What would that have done?"

Smiling at me Rachel's face is smug. "Men like to rescue women in distress and look at Mark. He's fussing over Sarah.My plan worked brilliantly."

" That wasn't because of your plan, just a lucky coincidence."

"Maybe, let's just see what happens next." My friend answers grinning walking to the table like she masterminded a great theft.

She laid down her dishes and took a seat by my father. I can see the table is arranged for eight people, not the usual ten. Looking around, the only free seats left are one at the end with Jacob and the last beside Ella. Moving to the spot by Jacob I am about to sit, when Ella speaks up.

"Andy, I'm saving that spot for your sister. Come sit next to me." I freeze, holding in a groan of despair following her order.

"Let Andy sit where she wants, Melissa is the one late." Father declares, giving me permission to sit where I desire. Ella glares at him, but thankfully she keeps her mouth shut. Breathing a sigh of relief I mouth to father a thank you.

"Thank the heavens, I did not want to sit next to your sister". Jacob whispers in my ear earning a chuckle from me."

I'm about to reply when a loud thumping is heard. Everyone quickly shoots out of their seats as the sound gets louder. I start trying to pinpoint its location but someone confirms it first.

"It is coming from outside" Sarah squeaks, jumping at each bang.

"Let me go find out what's going on." I volunteer to go to the door but a hand catches my wrist.

Jacob shakes his head refusing to let go of me. "I'll go." At that statement he pulls out his sword and gently removes me out of the way. Mark falls into the place behind him taking out his own weapon moving towards the disturbance.

Not wanting to be left out, I find myself following behind with Sarah and Rachel. As we get closer to the door, a male voice slurring curses can be heard.

I groan knowing who is causing this mayhem before Jacob opens the door. There, right on the grass outside the front door is a man in his late fifties. The man's pants are falling off him and his shirt stained. His brown hair is dirty and tangled like it hasn't been combed in days. Obviously he's drunk struggling on the ground with five soldiers restraining him. The soldiers look ready to beat the man senseless when he backhands one of them.

"You have no right to hold me." He yells flailing around like a three year old having a tantrum. "I pay my taxes" screaming when the soldiers finally tie his hands and legs together.

"Dad, please stop!" Sarah pleads hysterically, hurrying over to the man on the ground. She scans her father's face trying to detect injuries. "Good he isn't hurt" she says thankfully, though Rachel and I are disappointed.

John Palmer, upon hearing her voice stops his fighting turning his hateful gaze on his daughter. Instantly Sarah takes a step back and begins to tremble. Grabbing her hand, I squeeze it showing Sarah I'm here and she's safe.

"Sarah, where have you been?" He demands making her flinch.

"Andy's guest invited me over" she stutters nervously. "What are you doing here?" At that question everything goes downhill with John lunging for her. A soldier is luckily near jerking him back before he can lay a hand on Sarah.

"How dare you?" John curses. "Useless pig parading around not having my dinner on the table. I cannot wait to give you a thrashing when we get home." He threatens and once the words come out Rachel and I push Sarah behind us. Shielding her but an angry voice makes our efforts unwarranted.

"If you lay your finger on her. I'll beat you senseless" Mark warns marching outside to stand in front of John. John doesn't seem disturbed by Mark and only cackles until one of the soldiers slaps him across the face.

"You brutes. Wait until I get free. " Sarah's father screeches and for one sick second, I want the soldier to hit him again.

"Who is this waste of human flesh?" asks Mark crossley. I hesitated for a second, but the answer didn't come from me.

"This is John Palmer, Sarah's father, your Highness." Father declares standing beside me looking at John with disgust.

"Sarah's father, not much of one from what I witnessed." Mark scoffs, motioning for his men to pick John off the ground. Now face to face John and Mark look to be the same height, but the similarities stop there. The Prince's build is slender yet muscular, and John has a potbelly hanging off his fallen pants.

Grimacing, Mark orders his guards to secure John's pants to his body. Sighs of relief filled me because I didn't want to see his privates up close and personal.

"So, you're in charge of these idiots, boy," states John, spitting his words out. I am flabbergasted at the disrespect he is displaying. Mark is a noble, but John in his drunken state probably doesn't realize that.

"Yes, I am," Mark answers.

"Well get them to let me go. I need to take Sarah home and teach her a lesson about disobeying her father." John remarks, missing the lethal signs coming from Mark. The blow comes swiftly and hard with John landing on the ground in seconds. The stun soldiers have to help him back on his feet since he cannot get his bearings. Pushing his head up John has blood gushing from his nose. A sight I can't help but be happy to see. I didn't know how many times I saw Sarah with similar injuries without being able to do anything. Finally, karma is catching up to John.

"Try it and I'll have you arrested." Mark declares.

"I can do as I please with my daughter and no boy will stop me." John barks back and I hate to admit what he says is the truth. My father and grandmother tried numerous times to put him in jail. Yet he always got out because Sarah refused to press charges.

"This boy is the Crown Prince of Gallopia" Mark corrects John getting a look of fear from the man. "I can guarantee that you will not walk away from this one Mr. Palmer. Men go take him to jail" the prince orders as his men drag John away when a quivering voice yells out.

"Please, don't take him to jail." Sarah blocks their exit.

"Sarah, you cannot be serious." Mark shouts out letting his anger get the best of him but when she flinches he realizes his mistake. Cautiously he went to her and took her hand. "I cannot let him get away with trying to hurt you."

Looking up, Sarah stares at him with tearful eyes "He's my father Mark." The prince, at her words, studies her and turns to John begging on the ground.

"Please release me your Highness, I'm sorry" John begs.

"See he's sorry Mark, let me take him home" Sarah implores.

"Hell No!" Rachel hollers making Sarah jump into Mark's arms. "If Mark is letting him go, you will be going to my house where it is safe." Frowning, Sarah is about to disagree, but Mark interrupts.

"I agree with Rachel. If you want your father free to sober up, you must go to Rachel's house." He declares and when Sarah is not wavering so the prince adds. "If you don't agree, your father will be spending many nights in jail".

"Fine" Sarah submitting to Mark's terms.

"Men, take John to his house and make sure he sobers up." Mark commands his men and after saluting the soldiers pull John down the hill. It takes several minutes for everyone to settle down only when John is out of sight. Looking down Sarah clears her throat with big tears rolling down her face.

"I'm sorry, my father's behavior was horrible" she apologized in a fit of tears.

"Hey Sarah don't cry" Rachel says in a consoling voice. "Your father's behavior isn't your fault and no one blames you."

"He's my family; my burden" She mumbles stubbornly. " I need to go and clear my head." I shake my head at that answer knowing this is Sarah's way of withdrawing from her problems. Her father's behavior is a moot point in her life, something she learned to deal with a long time ago.

" Let me walk you to Rachel's house," Mark offers, with Sarah quickly refusing.

"No, it's fine, stay. Rachel can take me there." She answers shortly before walking away without any goodbye. I know she didn't mean the harshness in her voice and by tomorrow Sarah will apologize later.

"Sarah, wait up." Rachel yells running to catch up to Sarah giving us waves of farewells. Mark looks ready to pursue them if Jacob did not interfere.

"She needs time," He advised his friend softly.

" I can help if she lets me." Mark insisted, looking so concerned that I had to say something.

"Give her a day. Sarah usually needs time to process stuff like this." I explain.

"Alright, I will take your advice since you are her friend." Mark relents and yips when Jacob claps him on his back hard. "

Good, now let's get some food in you, slugger." Jacob says in a jolly mood directing his friend back into the house. After that only father and I are left outside going over all that happened.

"Now, that boy is a keeper" father announces once the royals are gone.

"Yes I agree, Sarah is in good hands with him" I reply feeling a weight lift off my shoulders. The uneasiness I was feeling about Sarah's wedding is leaving me by what I just witnessed. Seeing Mark defend Sarah was eye-opening making me realize that fate had it right; they belonged together.

"Andy, you look certain about that," father mentions with a knowing smile. "Did someone see something with her magic and didn't tell her old man?"

"I might have" I tease, earning an additional grin from my father. "I'm going to stay outside for a little longer. Go inside and keep our guests entertained before mother starts pestering them about marrying Mel."

"Oh dear I forgot about her" father scrambles running inside horrified. I can't blame him. Ella is relentless when it comes to obtaining her goals. Feeling a slight breeze, I decide to go to the path where my favorite flowers are growing. I wave to the guards around me climbing to the top of the hill and find the moonlight hitting my ideal spot overlooking the pink and yellow wildflowers.

Laying down in the grass it tickles my scalp, but I ignore it and let my body relax. The vision of Sarah is coming back to me, and I can't help but laugh. Who would have thought that Mel, the perfect child of the village, will be another Weston witch? And Sarah Palmer the drunkard's daughter will be a princess. Wait until all the villagers' who were rude to Sarah realize she will be royalty. Their mouths will be on the ground wishing they treated her better.

Remembering her smile in that wedding dress makes me grin. At least Sarah will be happy and not miserable, that is the important thing. I admit adjusting to her departure will be hard. Although one thing I learnt is the future is an unchangeable force, so all I can do is change with it.

Witnessing Mark protect Sarah from her father transformed everything that I was fighting. Having such a passionate and tender man is something Sarah deserves. And starting anew would be good for Sarah especially from Weston where her father's reputation is tarnished. In Gallopia, Sarah will be a Princess, with Mark to love her. There will be no one to tease her for having old clothes or make fun of her for having to work as a maid.

I'm sort of jealous of her for getting a chance to leave Weston. I know I should not be envious of my friend for escaping her life. Sarah is the sweetest person and finally fortune lands in her lap. Looking down at Weston my life isn't so depraved, but I always desired to see more lands.

Weston is a place where families are raised, and someday I want that. However I also sought to explore and meet different people. To travel and see a world that isn't like the one I recognize in my everyday life. Nonetheless everyone expects me to stay and take over my father's position one day. We the Millers are the caretakers of Weston for generations and that's my destiny.

Trying to think of something else I acknowledge after the festival it will be Rachel, Laura and me. I let myself shatter this time as tears ran down my face soaking my cheeks. I have less than two months to spend with one of my best friends until she is gone forever. Wiping my face feeling dumb for crying about the unavoidable. Thinking of my friends Laura, the sensible one of our group, will take the news better than Rachel .

My Native friend would probably make a joke to lighten our mood.. Laughing, I could see Laura trying to make things better by telling one of her terrible puns.

Trying to picture something funny, an image of my blond sister surfaces in my head. I giggle over how Mel will take the news that Sarah is marrying a prince. She'll probably scream and pull out her hair in one of her legendary fits.

Scratching my head, I wonder if I should tell Mel that I saw her future and it wasn't what she's expecting. The girl who dreams of wearing fancy dresses and living in a castle will be a housewife. It didn't come as a surprise to me that Mel didn't earn any royal approval. Truthfully, I have known her fate for a year now. I didn't mention it because I don't want to crush my sister's hope as she tries with mine.

Mel is an awful sister but still deserves happiness before she becomes Melissa Walker, the wife of Matthew Walker. Yes, Mel is the one that marries Matthew not me. When the vision first came I honestly laughed my hardest in relief and joy. All those times my sister teased and taunted me about being engaged to Matthew. But it is Mel who will marry that jerk, and I couldn't see a more perfect couple.

Losing track of time, I gaze up at the stars until a voice snaps me out of my daze.

"Can we speak in private, Andy?"

Mark appears next to me holding out his hand for me to grab. "Of course." I reply a little stunned, taking the offered hand, letting him pull me up. He points to the barn and leads the way as I try to dislodge flowers out of my hair. The curse of having curls is anything can get tangled in them I huff. Once in the barn he goes to one of the stalls and pets a horse leaving me to wonder what's all this about.

"Tell me about Sarah." He finally blurts out anxiously looking at me.

"What do you want to know?" I ask with a grin now knowing the reason why Mark wanted to speak. He's fishing for information about Sarah to romance her.

"Everything" he proclaims, making me laugh at his eagerness.

"Okay, she's seventeen and her birthday is November 10th" I divulge with Mark nodding at the information. I tell him her favorite color, foods and anything she likes. "Is there anything else you want to know that doesn't include her underwear?" I tease ignoring the laugh from him. And then his expression becomes harsher suddenly.

"Can you tell me about John?"

Tensing up I had a theory he was going to ask this. With a sigh I begin explaining the details I know. "John is a drunk who spends all the money he makes, and half of Sarah's on alcohol. He doesn't care about Sarah and treats her worse than dirt. He only wants her around to be his servant and if she doesn't do it, he hits her."

"Are you sure about that?" Mark questions looking ready to kill.

"Yes, Sarah always has an unexplained bruise, black eyes or broken bones. One day he beat her so severely, she limped for a week." I hiss, remembering seeing my friend trying to walk through her pain or cover her bruises.

"This doesn't make sense, why has your father not done anything about John?" Mark rage kicking the feed and spilling it. "He's the village leader, Andrew should have jailed that man. "

"My father has tried but Sarah will not turn on her father. And since John doesn't do it in public his hands are tied" I argue on my father's behalf.

"Why would Sarah do that? Protect John if her injuries are as severe as you tell me? Mark sounds frustrated and I can understand why.

"Sarah has a kind heart and cares for everyone, even if they hurt her. She wants to see the good in everyone and that is especially so for her father".

"I don't think there is any good in that man." Mark responds, taking a seat next to me. "I guess I have to speed up my plan now. There is no way I am leaving my future wife alone with that man."

"Future wife!" I squeal playfully, wiggling my eyebrows earning a grin from the prince.

Gone is the angry expression on his face as a happier one appears. "You're worse than Jacob," Mark laughs, shaking his head.

"Okay lover boy." I tease loving the blush of embarrassment I'm getting from Mark." How are you going to win my shy friend's heart?" Mark looked dumbfounded at my question. Did he not think of how he is going to get Sarah to fall for him. "You are a typical man with no sense of romance."

"I'm romantic" Mark contends" Look how I approached Sarah this evening, I did a brilliant job."

" Yes I saw you frighten her by kissing her hand in front of a crowd. Sarah hates being the center of attention." I warn pointing out his mistake.

"Well there go my plans to publicly propose at the festival." He mumbles in gloom and my mouth drops.

"You were planning on proposing to her in front of hundreds of people? Are you nuts?" I scream out knowing what a disaster that would have been. Sarah would have frozen up and been in tears from distress. " Sarah is a shy person, something small and intimate would be a better choice."

"Okay, small and personal is something I can manage." Mark says, smiling to himself. "I just want this to be perfect for her so she can fall in love with me. Sarah is my other half, the person the Tollar stone chose for me."

"You do not have to worry about her loving you. I got a good hunch that will happen. " I laugh thinking of my vision of their wedding and Sarah's happy face.

"I hope you're right Andy, but I wish I could take a glimpse at the future."

"Trust me knowing the future isn't all that great. " I express with a groan thinking about the trouble that comes with my magic.

"Talking from personal experience" Mark inquires?

"Yes, being a seer can be annoying to say the least. People always say they want to know their futures but when someone tells them they fight it. Life is meant for surprises, why spoil them with what will happen."

"Hmm, I guess I never considered it from that point of view."

"It is, and do not ask about your future, I don't take requests" I mumble. Mark seems to get the warning and changes the topic.

"Okay, tell me about yourself."

"What do you want to know?"

"Are you courting anyone?" Mark asks, getting a glare from me. "I wasn't asking for myself, just trying to get the topic going." He quickly corrects the misunderstanding and I nod not taking offense.

"Nope and I don't believe there will be anyone for a long time." I respond honestly not seeing myself in any romantic entanglement.

" Maybe the right man is just waiting close by," Mark says, smiling softly at me. His words were meant to be uplifting yet I cannot believe them. Ella is always in my head telling me no man will ever want me.

"It's okay, I knew a long time ago I wasn't a catch to men.." I state pointing to my dirty clothing as an example of my unworthiness. "I am not what most men want in a wife and I accepted that a long time ago."

"Hey, you are a great catch Andy" Mark argues. "You're pretty and with that red hair of yours, men are probably too dazzled to approach you."

"Then tell me why no boy has ever possessed the courage to ask me out." I mumble cynically. "I am not what men find attractive." I'm about to say something else when Mark starts to laugh uncontrollably.

"That's a load of crap." The prince snorts out, wiping tears from his eyes. "My soldiers have been staring at you since we first met."

"Really?"

Grunting Mark confirms the statement. "Yeah, Jacob even threatened to send them away out of jealousy." My mouth dropped at that revelation and my face must have shown it too. "I guess the foresight doesn't show you everything" he jokes, enjoying my dumbfounded expression. I can't comprehend what Mark just revealed about Jacob being interested in me. It has to be a mistake there is no way a royal could be remotely attracted to me.

The Kiss

11 What are you doing out here? " a male voice demands. Turning towards the voice, I see Jacob scowling at us for some unknown reason. I move away from Mark feeling strange to be in his presence now that Jacob's here.

"How did you come upon us without making a sound?" I ask deflecting the weird emotions I'm consumed with for the green eyed royal.

"My people specialize in stealth fighting." Jacob answers simply, moving his gaze from me to Mark. The stare was hostile but Mark didn't look bothered at all.

"My friend, we are not your enemy so silence isn't needed with us." Mark laughs, missing the look of suspicion on Jacob's face.

"Enemies can come in all forms," Jacob alleges, making Mark's face sour. I'm about to interfere when Mark shakes his head telling me not to get involved.

"I don't betray the ones I call friends so watch your allegations Jacob." Mark warns and the tension in the barn spikes. They both stared down the other for a couple minutes until Jacob let out a chuckle. Mark soon follows and they both look like old friends again not like two people fighting only moments ago.

"I am sorry Mark, I made an ass out of myself" Jacob apologizes.

"Yes, you did" Mark states but then asks. "What brings you outside anyway."

"Oh Andrew sent me to find you, he wants to discuss the Delianians with you."

"Yes of course" Mark jumps up giving Jacob a grin before returning his attention to me. "Sorry Andy, it looks like our time has come to an end, but it was nice talking to you."

"The same and please use that information I gave you for good not evil."

" I cannot make that promise" he quips before leaving out of the barn. Shaking my head at the comment I thought the man was an interesting choice for my shy Sarah.

"Did I interrupt a bonding moment between you two?" Jacob questions taking a seat on the barrel next to me.

"Yes, we are discussing wedding plans and me in a white puffy dress." I fib thinking I'll earn a chuckle but Jacob is not laughing..

" That's not funny."

"Fine. we were discussing his plan to ask Sarah to marry him."

Blowing a sigh of relief Jacob looks less tense. "Yes, that's much more logical than you and Mark."

"You don't think Mark would find me a suitable wife? " I ask, feeling a little insulted.

"You aren't compatible with each other. Mark needs someone who can support him and be his rock when he needs it the most" Jacob explains. "Gallopia is in crisis right now with the Delianians and he's under a lot of stress. Having a calm wife will ease some of his burdens from his shoulders."

"I never thought Mark had so many problems. He's always happy and carefree." I realize how much I misjudged the kind prince.

" He's good at masking his troubles, everyone does it, even you, Andy" he points out.

"True, although my issues are small compared to what is facing Weston right now."

"Weston's problems should be over soon, if Mark and Sarah marry" Jacob proposes.

"If my vision is right it will happen soon" I announce not caring I revealed that fact to Jacob.

" So That's what you saw earlier? Did you tell Mark?

"No," I comment, giving him a glare. "And neither of us are going to spill the beans. Let it happen naturally."

" Okay I will not reveal anything to Mark , I promise" Jacob pledges. "Although I don't get your anger from earlier about your vision. If they marry Weston, is saved. You should have been joyous, not the opposite."

" I was angry because Sarah will have to leave us for that future to happen. I couldn't accept that I'll lose one of my best friends to a stranger . However after seeing Mark stand up for her I knew this was the right path for Sarah."

"Are you sure? I know losing a friend is hard."

"Yes, it's time to let go and move on." I reply with a grin, but my face falls a little. "We aren't children anymore, and marriage is just a part of growing up. It isn't reasonable for us to always be together, especially if we are trying to build new lives. Very soon my friends will be off making new plans for themselves, and I will be here tending the fields."

"What about marriage for yourself?".

""My only marriage proposal was from Matthew Walker. You met his family today so that is a big NO."

"There might be someone else," Jacob suggested, making me roll my eyes.

"If this person likes me, hiding is not getting my attention."

"Okay if that's how you want it done" Jacob says, grabbing me by the shoulder forcing me to face him. " All day I've been dying to do this since I saw your face in the crowd."

Touching my face and tilting my head he pressed his lips against mine. Shock and overwhelm I remain still letting his lips move my own. My feelings from earlier come rushing back to me and almost naturally I wrap my arms around his neck. The sensation of his lips with my own is unbelievable. Now I know why Rachel is always going gaga over Cody's kisses. If they feel half as good as this I owe her a huge apology.

The kiss only lasts for seconds before we break apart. Not connected anymore questions begin flowing in my mind. How did Andy Miller, the girl who couldn't even get her hair untangled, end up kissing a prince? That is the idea I'm trying to process. It has to be a colossal joke one you hear about in rumors I theorize. Just when I make my mind up Jacob sweeps me back in his arms.

"That was good. Let's see if the second time is even better." 'He proclaims kissing me again.. I admit it was better than the first time, but I'm too mad to enjoy it.

"Is this a joke because I am not laughing" I accuse?

Raising an eyebrow Jacob looks confused. "You think this is a joke? I just kissed the girl I've been thinking about all day."

"Really that's a lie. Most of the time we've known each other you called me fire head!"

"Boys tease the girls that they like " Jacob comments, not in the least bit shaken.

"You aren't a schoolboy, and I am not a fool. Men of your pedigree don't go for a powerless seer like me" I hiss. " I bet this is a sport for you, to get a dumb village girl to fall for you but that isn't happening today." Yelling the last part tears rolls down my face. I'm about to flee when Jacob blocks my exit refusing to let me pass..

"Let me go," I growl.

"Andy, you're wrong and I do like you." He claims looking at me with his green eyes filled with honesty. " Something about you pulled me in when we met. And once I found out you're a seer it made sense."

"What does being a seer have anything to do with it?"

"Because my soulmate has the magic of knowing. And your father confirmed you're the only seer in this region of age to marry."

"The stone picked a seer for you to marry and now you're stuck with me." I grumble, not liking that Jacob is saddled with an ugly girl like me because of a magical stone's prediction.

"I know what you're thinking," he declares, grabbing my hands and pulling me back to him. "Yes. I do find you attractive, anyone with eyes can tell that."

Snorting, I can't help but grin at that statement." So you don't mind that I'm a little blunt and will question your decisions constantly. " I challenge him still not believing I'm what he wants as a wife but I get a surprise.

"Exactly, I want someone to tell me I'm wrong," Jacob agrees. " I never desire an agreeable wife but someone who can be my companion."

"I can't argue with insanity" I groan when Jacob closes the distance between us.

"Now that we have that settled. Let's get back to something more pleasant" he murmurs when our lips meet again. Losing myself in his warmth, I failed to notice footsteps coming our way until a gasp separated us.

There in plain view is my sister with a heartbroken look on her face. Concern, I move to talk to her, but Mel runs back to the house.. Tucking a fallen piece of hair out of my eyes I want to scream in embarrassment.

"Your sister has the worst timing." Jacob grumbles, not in the least bit humiliated, more annoyed at being interrupted.

I didn't know if I should slap him or kiss him, so I chose neither. "I've got to catch her before she tells my parents we were fornicating." I rush out ready to stop whatever damage Mel can inflict on my reputation..

Moving to walk past him Jacob takes hold of my hand. "Let's go together and explain it. That way people will get my side too."

Biting my lips, "I don't think it's a great idea to be seen together." I voice already knowing Ella wouldn't like the prince being at my side.

"Andy, what can it hurt? I'm not ashamed of what I was doing, are you?" Jacob questions and when I don't answer, his face drops. "Oh, I thought" he mutters so brokenhearted that I have to explain.

"I'm not ashamed but embarrassed." I clarify hoping that would settle his mind, but the frown remains. " Come on Jacob, I didn't mean to hurt your feelings."

"You didn't hurt my feelings" Jacob finally responds. "I just want you to feel the same way and I was wrong." In those words his deflated demeanor makes sense.

"I do like you Jacob," I confess. "I liked you from the moment I saw you, so don't give me those sad eyes." Grabbing his face I give him a peck on the cheek before dragging him to my home. "Come on, before I lose my nerve and rethink this plan of us facing Ella.." I mumble missing the grin on Jacob's face.

We walked hand in hand to the house only stopping when the guards bowed to us. When that happened it surprised me but I chose to ignore it. Right now my attention needs to be on saving my honor from my sister's lies.

Opening the door, we are met with a smiling Ella in a blue apron.. She looks like a charming hostess to anyone else, but the scowls Ella is sending me is the total opposite.. "Your Highness, it was nice of you to retrieve Andy." She says in an overly sweet voice."

Squeezing my hand "It was my pleasure." Jacob answers, giving me a grin earning a blush from me. With that, he led us into the house pulling me along as Ella scrambles to catch up.

Heading to the table he takes a seat and motions for me to do the same. Afterward he places our conjoin hands-on display for all to see. Jacob isn't being coy and is shoving our mutual attraction in Ella's face.

"Would you like some of the cake that Melissa baked?" She mumbles out giving me a menacing glance .

"Yes, I will have a slice." Jacob replies, giving Ella a level stare back . He must have noticed her treatment of me making my mother back off. Curtsying she goes into the kitchen to grab the cake. "That could have gone better" He groans rubbing his head in worry.. He keeps flicking his hands against the table nervously until he finally stops. " Andy, what I'm about to do I need you to keep an open mind about it." He sounds uncertain, making me feel the same emotion with a little anxiety.

"Jacob, what's going on?" I state before being interrupted by Ella coming back. Frowning at the disturbance Jacob did not seem happy by her presence as she served him the cake.

"I know you'll enjoy this cake. Mellissa is an excellent cook" Ella boasts, laying it on thick. Rolling my eyes, I long to tell Jacob I baked the cake and Mel cannot cook to save her life. Her idea of cooking is burning water on the kettle and calling it tea.

"Mother, where is Mel?" I ask wanting to know if Mel told her about what happened in the barn.

"In her room like a proper young lady should be." Ella replies by sending me a scathing look and I know Mel told her what she saw.

I'm about to defend myself when a chair falls over. "I can't wait any longer," Jacob says, standing up and bowing in front of us formally. "Ella, you are the lady of the house," He starts in the most respectable way possible. "I would like to propose marriage to your daughter."

Our expression of awe is the only answer he gets for a response. My mind is racing, Jacob just proposed to me "

Yes, of course, Melissa will be thrilled" Ella recovers first to answer. A smile of triumph fills her face as Ella sneers at me like she won a victory.

"I think you are mistaken on which daughter I'm asking for. "Jacob asserts not to please that my mother thought this was for Mel.

"You do mean Melissa right?" She asks, puzzled . At that statement I actually believe Ella thinks she only has one daughter. Since in her logic I'm not fit to be called her child in any way or form.

"No, I mean Andy's hand in marriage." He announces loudly making it clear to her.

"This is very unexpected. I must speak to Andrew first" Ella stammers looking pale for a minute. The comment about father is new since she was ready to accept for Mel without his approval. What's the difference in my case I wonder, is this her way of ruining my chance of royalty?

My presumption is proven correct when her face morphs into a smirk. "Your Highness, Andy cannot be your bride. She is already promised to Matthew Walker."

"What" I shout out when hearing the outrageous lie.

"Andy, why did you not tell him of your marriage with Matthew. I'm ashamed of you for leading this man on." She continues like I'm the one lying. Taking a sympathetic stare she looks at Jacob motherly. "I am sorry for Andy neglecting to tell you of her engagement, but her sister is still an option."

"I'm not engaged to that fool, and you know it." I challenge furious that Ella has the gumption to fabricate such a colossal lie.

"How dare you speak to me like that." She hollers her blue eyes locked on me. "You should be happy that a boy wants to marry an unsuitable girl such as yourself." Her insult didn't bother me more than the falsehood she alleged against my character.

" Ella that's enough" Jacob orders glowering at Ella making her blanch in fear. " Andrew told me no marriage contract has been made for Andy, you're lying."

At this Ella's confidence is gone now that her scheme has fallen apart. "It isn't in writing yet but the boy Matthew and I have discussed the matter." She stumbles out and everything from earlier makes sense now with Cody's words. My so-called mother was planning to wed me off without telling me.. " I believe the match of Andy and Matthew is beneficial for both. Andy is not a lady and Melissa is more qualified to be your wife."

"Your opinion on the matter is worthless. I made my decision so stop trying to change my mind." Jacob growls but Ella still looks determined to argue." If you continue Ella, I'll report you for violating the Princess Festival rules."

" Please don't" she pleads, looking terrified at paying the penalty. One hundred gold coins is a small fortune to us in Weston and to most commoners. A steep punishment so people will not interfere in the choosing process for royals. Looking into his eyes, I wonder if Jacob is bluffing. The feedback I get from them isn't faltering and Ella recognizes that too.

" I will if I see anymore meddling from you" Jacob warns.

"Understood, let me go get Andrew for you." She stutters fleeing the room leaving only silence in her wake. At her departure everything comes crashing down around me. He proposed marriage which I cannot refuse. The penalty of the Princess Festival is law, one I can't go against so I must submit.

Groaning silently, I completely forget Jacob is still in the room until he touches me. " I'm glad I got the proposal out of the way it was driving me crazy."

"You are crazy" I dispute.. "You just proposed marriage there is no way of taking that back." I look at him not understanding his motives? "We just had our first kiss. Jumping into marriage is not logical."

" I regret nothing?"

"A marriage proposal should take longer to consider, like *years!*" I scream freaking out about being married to Jacob. I'm going to be a royal which means I'll have to leave my family and friends behind. Shaking at the mere idea, a hug soothes my nerves as Jacob wraps himself around me.

"Andy, remember to keep an open mind." He says to me waiting for my composure to return before he starts again. "Andy, my whole life I dreamed of someone who doesn't desire the glamor of royalty. Someone who does not believe they are better than others. The girl I searched for doesn't mind tackling the annoying stuff. I want someone who isn't afraid to handle budgets with me and solve problems by my side. I don't desire a pampered princess but a partner beside me."

Feeling the tears run down my face I can't help but grin. Everything he said is something I wished for in a husband. I just never guessed someone would want the same thing. Still, there are misgivings" You wouldn't mind a wife who wears pants more than you" I question.

"I do not care about that" Jacob answers. "In Polla women wear whatever they desire and are warriors."

"Really?" I reply a little amazed at how progressive Polla is to Perta. Even in my land women can be leaders but aren't allowed to fight.

"Yes, my cousin Priscilla is one of them."

"Are you really sure about marrying me?" I ask, again my doubts emerging." I am not gorgeous like Rachel or Mel and I certainly don't have their power."

"I don't care about appearances much" Jacob verbalizes. "My mother was disfigured from a cougar attack at the age of ten and my father accepted her. What matters is the person's soul and yours is honest."

At that speech he clears my qualms away and my mind skips to something else. Leaving Weston behind will be scary and going to be the hardest challenge I ever faced. Yet being a seer I know destiny doesn't wait for us to decide.

Grandma Ruth

After the proposal settles in my head I start to smile in excitement. I'm finally going to see a land other than Perta and explore it.. My wish of leaving Weston is happening and all my doubts vanish. At that moment, I make my decision and realize something important is missing in the proposal.

" Where is my ring?" I ask frowning at not being presented one. Every girl deserves her engagement ring and I'll be damned if I did not get one.

"In Polla, with my advisor it's a family heirloom" Jacob answers, missing my words entirely. He did not comprehend that I just accepted his proposal.

"When are we leaving?" I try again smiling at the man that will be my husband.

"In two months" he replies finally understanding. "Are you saying you will marry me without a fight?"

I gaze at him before speaking, "The festival rules are a witch can't deny a claim on her. Nonetheless, if you want to die at an early age from stress, why would I refuse."

Chuckling he leans down to kiss me. "Thank you and even if the festival wasn't forcing the wedding on you. I wouldn't have stopped trying. Andy, I've wanted you since I touched the stone eight years ago".

A warm feeling consumes me thinking about the man holding onto me. "Jacob, I think I might love you" I confess.

"I love you too," he whispers, making me cry. I never heard anything so sweet before but we have things to discuss.

"Okay lover boy, we need to discuss my new Kingdom. And what my duties will be in Polla." I demand putting some distance between us.

Sighing at my action Jacob starts to explain things. "Polla is different from Perta, we haven't had peace in decades" he stresses to me. "Andy, you will be part of a kingdom that has a militia in every village and city. The people, even the women, can swing a sword with the best of men".

"Polla is in a war state." I respond by taking notes in my head." What about the people and the environment? "

"Our people are wonderful, right down to the last child. In my land we have two different courts of law to keep order. The first court is the Commoner Court and the other the Superior Court. " At that, I'm impressed hearing about their judiciary system. "As for the environment, we don't have many farmlands like Perta. Most of our food comes from the trading post and Perta crops. Polla's terrain is largely dryland and mountains, but our people adapted to it."

I want to ask more questions, but a loud baritone voice enters the room. "I hear that my twin got proposed too, is this true?" I turn towards the source of the voice.

Father comes barreling up to me with Ella following. My father has a wide grin showing on his face and Ella looks like she swallowed a lemon. Not taking heed of her unhappiness I gave my father a hug. "Yes, I did get a proposal. Now you have to get someone else to bargain with Mrs. Moore" I prod him a little.

"Nope, I'll just ship her off with you." He quips, making us both chuckle but this is short lived.

"Andrew " Ella screeches at the top of her lungs. "Tell the Prince that Matthew Walker has proposed to Andy, and she isn't available." Her demands fall on deaf ears as my father just frowns at the lie.

"Andy isn't engaged to Matthew, you know that Ella" he argues.

"His father asked for the two to marry."

"And I did not accept" father disputes.

"But" she stammers, not being able to say anything to manipulate the situation. Rolling my eyes, at her foolishness at thinking my father would ruin an alliance for her selfish dreams. Defeated Ella starts to whimper and cry falling on the floor making a scene. "She's going to ruin everything Andrew " she weeps. " I worked tirelessly to make Melissa into a perfect lady. And now it's all pointless because the prince chose that brash, sharp tongued tomboy."

I didn't know what to say, but Father did. Reaching for his wife on the floor he forces her to stand up. 'Listen Ella" he declares with his hazel eyes fierce with anger. "I have listened as you demean my child for years but you will not take this from her.. Andy's perfect the way she is and if you cannot accept that fact remain silent." Releasing Ella, he ignores her crying to change the topic. " Now my twin, we have to tell your grandmother the news."

"Father she probably already knows." I predict because my grandmother is a seer too.

"You're correct my dear" announces an older voice. Walking in is a woman in her sixties wearing a gray skirt and green shawl that highlights her hazel eyes. Her red hair is streaked with gray but still has the same brightness as her son and granddaughter.

Ruth Miller is still one beautiful woman even though her face might have a couple of wrinkles. People always say I look like a younger version of grandma, but I can't see it. Ruth has a womanly figure, and my boyish figure is nothing like hers.

"I cannot believe what I foresaw finally occurred." Grandma squeals, giving me a strong embrace.

"You saw this Mother and didn't warn me?" Father whines, giving his mother an annoyed scowl.

"What's the fun of knowing if you cannot see your loved ones' surprise faces." Grandma answers ending that conversation before father can get another word in. "Let's celebrate with cake and wine. Ella go get Melissa, so we all can congratulate Andy's engagement." I notice now my mother is off the ground glaring at grandma.

Groaning, I can see they're heading into one of their fights. Grandma and Ella never liked each other, which makes things awkward at family gatherings.

"Melissa cannot come down, she's sick" Ella lies. Trying not to seem bothered I know the real reason Ella is deceiving grandma. Mel will have a temper tantrum hearing of my engagement which would be embarrassing for Ella.

"She didn't look sick earlier." Mark states coming from the sitting room with a grin. "I heard the good news," he says, patting Jacob's shoulder and giving me a hug. "Told you he likes you."

My mouth opens and then I laugh realizing Mark was hinting about this earlier in the barn. "Fine I'm blind to love but I cannot wait to hear how you'll propose to Sarah." I announce poking fun at Mark whose face is red now..

"Oh, so this is the man who is going to marry my Sarah." Grandma says in an excited voice. Her hazel eyes scan Mark from his face to his toes admiring his body. "My girl is fortunate to have such a strapping lad for her future husband."

"Thank you, but I don't think we have been introduced." Mark responds by giving grandma one of his charming grins.

"Oh, a charmer, " grandma giggles. "I'm Ruth Miller but call me Grandma everyone else does. I can see you are as gorgeous as I saw in my vision of yours and Sarah's wedding."

"Grandma" I yell out not wanting her to reveal anymore.

"Don't be a party-pooper." Grandma says dismissing my concerns. "You have already seen the wedding with your magic." And with that Mark grin from ear to ear looking at me to confirm my grandma's statement.

"Yes, I saw your wedding to Sarah with my foresight." I admit but a shout afterwards nearly shatters my eardrums.

Howling in rage, Ella gives a hateful stare at grandma. "It's not true! He cannot marry Sarah!" .

"Ella, my sight is never wrong. This Prince is for Sarah, and only her."

"But, Melissa?" but before her sentence is completed. Grandma divulges the news I was hiding for a year.

"Melissa isn't going to marry a prince, Ella. She'll marry Matthew Miller and have two children by him." She declares her eyes glowing with magic.

A massive weight is off my shoulders now that Grandma revealed the vision. Ella is nasty on a good day. Hearing this, she would be horrible to the bearer of the news.

"You, lying bag of bones!" Ella screams, lunging for Grandma's neck. Luckily father grabs her before she can reach the older woman. In his arms she still tries to get at grandma acting more like a feral cat than a human. " I always knew you despised me but to makeup such a falsehood is underhanded. It's unbelievable to think my precious baby would be stuck with that stupid boy."

When hearing these words, I cannot believe her logic. She's adamant that Matthew is a great choice for me. Yet if the roles are reversed and Mel is to marry Mathew then he's unsuitable. "It's true. Mel will marry Matthew. I saw it a year ago with my magic too." Confirming grandma's account of the vision.

"Jealousy" Ella denies our statements again. "That's what you all are."

"Ella, please calm down," Father says in a reasonable tone.

"*Melissa, Melissa, Melissa*" Ella hollers over and over.. Watching her lose all sense of control was a frightening sight. No amount of consoling is working as she continues to act like a madwoman.

Finally, the mayhem ends as my sister walks into the room. Mel's appearance is the first thing I notice when she enters.. Her once sparkling blue eyes are red from crying and her face is puffy.

"What's the matter mama?" Mel asks, coming over to Ella.

Feeling Mel's support, Ella's whole demeanor changes. "Darling, these people think you will marry Matthew Walker." She accuses and Mel's mouth drops before my sister chuckles thinking this is a joke.

" That's Andy's future husband, I'm destined to marry a royal." Mel vows, lifting her chin to everyone in the room.

"You hear that everyone" Ella taunts. " Melissa will become a princess and Andy a hillbilly's wife."

"That's right, I'm the important one, not her." Mel says, giving me a nasty smirk. I really yearn to punch her, but someone interferes before an altercation can occur.

Looking angry Grandma appears fed up "Andy is just as important as you Melissa. And let's not forget she got a royal on her own merit, not you."

"He'll see the truth soon grandma." Mel asserts winking at Jacob who ignores her attempts at flirting..

"Child, that nasty demeanor of yours will land you in trouble one day." Grandma remarks looking at my sister in a knowing way which means it's a prediction..

"Shut up, old woman. I never liked you and your endless comments about destiny." Ella rages as Mel goes suddenly quiet out of fear at Grandma's words.

"Oh, it's breaking my heart" grandma laughs. "I made it no secret I disliked you Ella, especially seeing how you treat Andy. However, take this warning Ella, your ambition will be your downfall one day."

Snorting Ella only sneers at my grandma. "Your warning doesn't scare me Ruth. " At that statement Ella turns to my sister. " Let's go, we've spent too much time talking about these disappointments. We'll find a Prince who isn't blind to true beauty." And with that she swoops out of the room with a worried Mel following her. The only change in my sister is when she reaches me.

Her blue eyes are blazing with anger." This is not over sister" bumping into me when she leaves. I watch them go and I cannot say

I'm unhappy because the mood changes in the room. The uneasy atmosphere is gone and everyone sighs in relief. It takes some time before father has the men jolly again offering them glasses of wine. I sat with Grandma Ruth discussing what happened and my relationship with my sister.

"Sadly dear, I don't see that changing anytime soon" she says honestly.

"What is it about me that they hate so much?"

"Maybe it runs in the family," Grandma points out. " Ella has hated me since she met your father."

"Why is that?"

"I know all your mother's darkest secrets. Ones that if they get out will ruin her reputation and make her the lowest pariah in the village." My mouth drops at the information my Grandma just revealed. I'm about to ask about Ella's secrets but Grandma is tight lipped. "Don't ask my dear. Some secrets will come out in their own time. It is not for us to rush them". She explains and suddenly her eyes turn white because of magic.

"Sweetie you may want to duck." Grandma warns pushing herself and me to the ground just as a plate flies over our heads.

"What the?" I began to curse but an enraged howl caught my attention..

"Andy, you are a selfish brat" Mel screams running at me with another plate in her hand.

Shattered Dreams

Stunned, I lay on the ground like an idiot after almost being hit by my sister. Mel, seeing me frozen, tries to attack me on the ground. Thankfully my fiancé has quicker reflexes pulling me away so my sister collides into the floor not me. She moans loudly in pain at her fall. I smile in satisfaction at the outcome but curiosity is needling me for answers. Grabbing Mel by the shoulder, I jerk her up from the floor.

" Mel what the hell." I demand securing both of her hands around her back to stop further attacks against me.

"You had it coming for taking a prince for me." Mel accuses struggling, attempting to break free of my grip. Squirming away she put some distance between us.

"I didn't take Jacob away. He chose me."

"You seduced him, I saw you in the barn" Mel alleges .

" He was the one that kissed me first!!"

"This is not fair," Mel screams out, pulling her hair. "I'm the one that studied table manners and looked perfect everyday for years. You did none of that and still got a royal not me. How is that right you know nothing about being a royal but I do."

"All the things you mention Melissa are things I can teach Andy myself." Jacob interrupted wrapping his arms around me. "Although I can't teach kindness, something you lack in abundance.

His presence turns Mel's rage into confusion and despair. "I'm the beautiful one, why pick *her over me*?"

"I believe Andy is just as beautiful as you" Jacob counters back.

"Huh?" Mel laughs pointing at me. "That isn't beauty, just a mess of red tangles." At her remark I try to tame my frizzy curls but Jacob stops me instantly.

" Andy's beauty isn't just her physical appearance which I love, but her soul. She is a person my people can come to with their problems. Someone who will not buy every dress that my trust can fund. I don't want a shallow woman like you at my side. I need someone I can lean on when things get tough."

"Those aren't the duties of princesses." Mel yells looking at Jacob from head to toe like he is a foreign creature. "However, if you desire a princess like *that.* I can transform into that woman better than my sister ever can."

"Well, it's a moot point because I am not even a prince so I can't make anyone into a princess." Jacob reveals to my sister and everyone in the room.

"What!" I scream in dismay at the confession feeling confused. Jacob isn't a prince, but that doesn't make any sense? All day he acted like royalty and didn't refute the claim until now.. Was this all a huge joke to trick me into falling for him?

"I knew it" Mel shouts triumphantly, her whole face lighting up with a grin. "I knew something was suspicious with him. And now I know why he didn't even bother to look at me. He isn't even a prince or real royal, that's why he went for Andy.. You thought you were the important one sister" she mocks. "But all you got was a pretender who was looking for an affair with a simpleton, and you fit the bill."

I'm speechless, unable to argue my sister's claims. "Melissa. That is enough" Father scolds looking in anger at Mel bullying me. I try to block out what they're saying. All I can do is stare at Jacob and wonder how he can do this to me. Why make me think he loves me and then lie straight to my face?

"No, Father, I'm not done," Mel delivers, giving Jacob another arrogant stare. "Pretending to be a prince is pathetic and Andy should be proud to get what you have to offer her, *nothing.*"

"If you let me finish my statement from before. I'm not Prince Jacob, but *King* Jacob the first. And that will make your sister a Queen when we marry." He announces with some smugness in his voice.

I did not know who was more speechless Mel or I. I look around the room and see Mark grinning. And Grandma even has a smile on her face telling me this is true.

"I'm going to be a queen" I whisper..

"Yes, you will be Queen, but first we have an issue." Jacob responds a little perplexed. " We need to think of calling you something other than Andy in the Royal court."

"Just call her Andrea," Grandma suggests. "It's the name I was going to pick for her father if he was a girl."

"Mother!".

"What, it was after your late Aunt Andrea" Grandma replies, making father shake his head.

"Yes, I like the sound of Andrea, and I think it will work." Jacob answers before looking at me. "What do you say, it's still close to your original name?"

"Yes, but I still want Andy for a nickname." I demand not negotiating on that part. Andy has always been my name and I want to keep it that way in some form. Jacob agrees with the bargain, making me happy.

"She is going to be a Queen? The girl that ran around as a boy most of her life? How does that make sense to anyone? " Mel growling now that Jacob's true status is out. "Andy doesn't have anything to offer your kingdom but her eyes. I'm an earth witch that can make you money, so choose me instead."

I'm about to speak but Grandma shakes her head. "Let Melissa dig her own grave ." I bit my tongue, remaining silent letting my sister continue her rant.

"I'll be a great queen, and an even better wife." Mel says swaying her hips trying to seduce Jacob who seems disturbed by her display. Her actions are showing everyone her true character, there's no redemption after this for her.

"Melissa, leave right now before you disgrace our family anymore!" Grandma orders pulling Mel away from Jacob.

"Why, so your favorite granddaughter can have what should have been mine from the beginning?"

Rolling my eyes, this is classic Mel. When things don't go her way, she has to blame someone else. It was projecting or diverting the responsibility to someone else's shoulders.

"Melissa, I treated you and Andy the same all your lives" Grandma argues.

"Liar! Andy was always your favorite. And now she gets to be a Queen and gets to live in a castle." Mel cries. "I have always wanted this, and now I will have no one to marry."

"Melissa, we will talk about this later in private." Father says, trying to calm my sister down.

"Why? So, you can say everything will be alright. That I'll still get married to Matthew?"

"Melissa, it has already been decided by fate," Grandma declares.

"Grandma, you think marrying Matthew is a good future!"

"I think Matthew is a fine boy for you." Heads turn to our red-haired father who made that comment.

"Why?" Mel mumbles in tears.

"Matthew is a stable young man who comes from a good family. He's one of the most sought-after bachelors in the village" Father praises and his brows go up, something he does when he has an idea. "And we can finally link our family to the Walker's with your marriage."

"Daddy no" Mel begs looking horrified and I can't blame her. The way our father is talking he seems set on making the match even if Mel disagrees.

"Maybe we should discuss this later." I intervene and Mel nods in agreement eagerly.

"No, I believe this is brilliant. Tomorrow I'll arrange the marriage with Tim Walker." Father announces leaving no room to argue with his decision.

I didn't know Mel could shriek that loud." Mother, mother" she hollers over and over. The meltdown makes everyone go quiet as Mel continues to screech.. It isn't long when running footsteps come our way.

"What's going on? " A panic Ella burst into the room and saw Mel in tears. "Baby, don't cry, mama's here now." She says soothingly, repeating the mantra until Mel calms down.

"Mama, the man you married" Mel barks out glaring at our father with hatred. "Ordered me to marry Mathew Walker."

"What?" Ella explodes in anger with a white glow surrounding her. A chill enters the room and looking at my mother I knew she activated her magic. The aura around her is the only real warning when the door flies open.

A gale of wind comes into the house knocking over paintings and shattering vases. The noises seem never-ending as I wrap my arms around my chest as the temperature drops suddenly. Jacob hands his coat over to Grandma who is shaking from the chill. Ella's outburst is getting out of hand when a bookcase nearly lands on Father.

"Ella, calm down before you destroy our house!" Father commands shielding his face from the harshness of the wind.

"Why should I listen to you when you're trying to ruin Melissa's future?" She shouts, throwing up her hands making a mighty gust of wind flipping our table. My mouth hangs open as our cedar table breaks from the impact on the floor. Ella just destroyed one of her favorite belongings.

"Mama, stop! You're scaring me" Mel stutters trembling on the floor. At the sound of my sister's voice, the wind slows and the aura vanishes around Ella.

Worriedly, Ella runs towards Mel wrapping her arms around my sister. Her magical energy finally disperses when her concentration is on Mel "I'm sorry I scared you baby," she apologizes, kissing Mel's head. "Go to your room. I'll be there shortly." Nodding her head, Mel walks out of the room without hesitation. Waiting for Mel to depart, Ella snarls at everyone remaining in the room. "Mark my words, I will not let you rob my daughter of an opportunity to become royalty."

"A prince will never choose her Ella, face the truth" Grandma grunts out..

"And why not? She's princess material" Ella maintains looking around the room before her eyes stop on Mark. "Tell me why you would pick Sarah over my daughter. Melissa is clearly the prettier girl of the two of them."

Mark glares at Ella at her statement. "Some things can't be learned, and class is one of them" he says in a manner only a prince can. "Your daughter's actions spoke volumes about hers. And my dear lady, so did you at this moment." Gasping at the insult Ella looks slighted and flies into a rage focused on me now.

"*You rotten girl*! She points at me accusingly.

"What did I do?" Dumbfounded how her rage suddenly turns from Mark to me.

"I know this is your fault somehow and I won't stand for it." Ella states raising her hand to slap me, but I grab it before she makes contact. I don't remember who made the first move. However it ends with my mother on her bottom as I stand over her. Feeling a slight sting in my hand, I'm stunned I hit Ella in self-defense.

"Andy, are you all right?" Jacob asks me. Still in a daze it takes Mark snapping his fingers in my face to wake me up.

"I hit my own mother" I croak out tears swelling in my eyes. I'm a horrible person. I just hit the woman who gave birth to me. To make matters worse Ella rises from the ground holding her cheek.

"I put a curse on you" she shouts, her eyes glowing. "I'll do everything in my power to ruin you.." Turning to look at the other occupants she promises. "Melissa will become royalty one day and those who stand against us are our enemies. I will guarantee that fact."

I didn't know if it's the coldness of her voice or my magic forewarning me of something. At that moment, I can see whatever civil relationship we once had is now finished.

Jacob comes to the same conclusion ushering me out of the front door. "I hate that woman," he mutters once we are safely outside and away from prying ears.

"Don't say that, she's still my mother."

"No mother is that horrible Andy" Jacob points out to me. " She put a curse on you out of jealousy.

"He's right I hate that blond banshee." Grandma grumbles behind me seeing that the others had followed us out except for Ella.

" I shouldn't have slapped her." I groan." Maybe if I had pushed her away things would not have gotten this far."

"None of this is your fault Andy. It's all on your mother" father says reassuringly.

"But" I try to say but Jacob swings me around to face him.

"It isn't your fault Andy. You defended yourself against an unprovoked attack by your mother. And I've got a feeling this fight has been coming for a long time.

"You're right Jacob but I've still got to live with my mother." I respond thinking about how miserable Ella is going to make my life. The extra chores and mean remarks will be endless.

"I can get you a room in the inn that I am staying at." Jacob offers but I decline.

"People will think it is indecent since we aren't married yet." I claim knowing that most of the villagers are traditional. Many of them feel that a woman shouldn't stay under the same roof as her fiancé.

"Stay with me" Grandma volunteers. "That way you get away from Ella and I can help you get ready for the festival."

"Really" I squeal in excitement.

"Yes, it will be like the sleepovers we had when you were little" grandma says. "And we can even invite Sarah to stay since going back to her father isn't an option anymore." I'm not going to even ask her how she knew about Sarah's living situation. Nothing surprises my grandma with her magical eyes.

"Well it settled my twin. You'll live with your grandma until you depart from Weston." Father declares and it all hits me at once. These next two months will be the last I have with family and friends. People who stuck with me even when I made a fool out of myself. I start to breathe heavily and sweat pours down my face from the dread I'm feeling.

"Andy, are you all right?" Jacob asks, seeing my reaction. " Is it about your mother?"

"It's got nothing to do with Ella" I reassure him about that. "It's about what will happen after the festival with me leaving Weston.

"Oh, I guess having two months to get your affairs in order is a little alarming." At that I nod confirming the accuracy of his statement." It is a lot to lose but look at what there is to gain" he claims.

"I lose my friends and family, to start over in a place where everything will be new." I rush out, getting my worries out in the open. "What am I gaining by leaving?"

"You gain a handsome King that thinks the world of you." He contends bringing me in closer for a peck on the lips. "And the rest we will deal with together."

"Okay" I agree, staring back at my house, knowing after today I won't come back. I will no longer be welcome here and honestly I don't care. This home is filled with pain and misery. Let Ella and Mel keep it.

"Let's go honey, it's past my bedtime." Grandma yawns yanking my arm and with that I'm on the path forward. Refusing to look back,

I match her steps and focus on something tangible. Pressure on my freehand gives me that feeling when Jacob encompasses it. Grinning, I knew everything would be all right and even if it wasn't. I still had him by my side for now on.

Rachel's Problems

The last two months went by quickly living with Grandma and I'm at my happiest. I'm away from Mel and Ella's attitude which is the biggest change in my life. And since the little fiasco at my old home, Sarah moved in with Grandma as well.

She seems less scared and smiles easier after leaving her father. And that new fancy piece of jewelry on her left hand didn't hurt one bit. A sparkling diamond cut ring in an oval shape with a gold finish was every girl's dream ring.

Sarah fainted when she saw the ring. It took Mark and myself several minutes to revive her, and she yelled yes to the proposal. I feel my eyes water, it was such a mushy moment I still want to cry. And that wasn't the only thing that changed over the last couple of months. Jacob and I have been spending our time together, and it's been lovely. He's funny and has a dry sense of humor that only few can get. And he used it well, especially on Matthew Walker when he came up to us one day a month ago.

That day I was assigned by my father to be in charge of the food for the festival. My fabulous fiancé insisted it would be funny to take my notepad. He held it above my head until I agreed to kiss him. I wanted to kick him in the shins but decided to give in.

I kissed him on the cheek, but Jacob wasn't having that. As soon as I was close enough he swooped me into his arms and brought me into a toe-curling kiss. I admit I probably would have seen Matthew walk up if I wasn't too occupied.

"Andy, what the hell?" Matthew bellows, causing everyone to turn toward us and for Jacob and me to pull away from each other. Marching up to us Matthew looked downright pissed staring at Jacob and me.

"Who is this Andy, why are you kissing him?"

Before I could speak, Jacob decides to meet Matthew halfway with a smirk. "I am King Jacob of Polla, and as for why I am kissing her, why not?" The challenge in his voice was clear. The people watching stood shocked and quiet, none more than Matthew.

Gone was his bravado and now his face looked scared. "She is my fiancée, your Majesty" he muttered so quietly I almost missed it, but the crowd before him gasped.

"I don't believe you about the engagement. Andy would have told me of a marriage contract" Jacob alleges, lifting an eyebrow. When Matthew looked down, refusing to answer, he began to smile. "No contract then and I have already spoken to Andrew Miller. He informed me there was never such an agreement."

"It was in discussion." Matthew barked fuming now that Jacob has successfully destroyed his claim. .

"I heard her father turned down the proposal, how is that in discussion?" Jacob asked, giving that cocky smirk that I hated when I first met him. I had to admit it was lovely when someone else was on the other side of it. Matthew faltered and Jacob continued.. "You lost. Get over it and leave my fiancée alone. And next time try having a tantrum with someone of your own age group." Looking around Jacob points to a young boy who couldn't be more than five digging in his nose. "He seems more your speed but when he learns to read. You might want to try a baby." Seeing the remark hit home. Jacob escorted me away from the drama with a grin.

After that day when I ran into Matthew, he shied away from me like I have a disease. Which is funny and rather enjoyable now that I don't have to deal with him again. Now it's the day of the festival we all decided to meet at the Riverside Inn.

The inn is a three-story Victorian with white trim, brown brick and ivy vines with pink lilies hanging around the windows. It's a picturesque place and the owner, Mrs. Seymour, made the inn into a success. The sixty-year-old woman would scrub someone's feet and likely chew their food for them. Anything it took for guests to have an enjoyable experience at her place. Walking in I see my friends sitting at a table in the corner. Waving, I go upstairs where Jacob's room is located on the second floor. Climbing the stairs, I straighten the new dress that Grandma bought for me. It's green, an excellent choice to highlight my red hair and it squeezed my waist showing off my shape. My bust is accented with a green topaz necklace my Grandma gave me. The stares I got on the street were pleasant, but I wondered what my betrothed would think.

Knocking on the door I'm nervous and bursting at the seams. What if Jacob thinks I look stupid or not beautiful and calls off the engagement. I'll be a laughing stock. I panic just when he opens the door.

Now I know how those men felt staring at me. There, in front of the door stands my shirtless King with a sleepy gaze. "Andy, it's a little early to be up my dear?" He yawns, moving aside to let me enter but I remain in the same spot. A silly grin spreads across my face happily while staring at his manly chest.

Frowning, he follows my gaze and realizes what got my attention. Jacob rolls his eyes pulling me inside before shutting the door. "Would you stop staring at my chest?" He grumbles looking self-conscious which makes me grin more. Who knew this cocky king is uncomfortable with his own appearance.

"Sorry but I can't help it" I laugh.

"That is easily fixed." Jacob says putting on a clean shirt remedying the situation. Once fully clothed did he continue speaking. "Now why did you show up early?"

"Are you kidding, these are my last days in Weston. I'm going to enjoy them, not sleep in or be lazy." I declare urging Jacob out of the door. " Come on, our friends are waiting downstairs with breakfast."

Grumbling is the only response I get as I shove Jacob in the hallway. Hurrying downstairs to the dining room of the Inn we see most of the guests eating their breakfast.. The large room is filled with dozens of people but luckily our friends are easy to spot. Their table has an assortment of mouthwatering foods for breakfast. .

Taking the seat next to Rachel, I immediately dug in, fixing myself a plate. "You must be hungry today." Rachel observes wiping my face with a napkin.

" I didn't eat before I came here." I reply by taking a bite of the bread before adding. "What did we miss?"

"I was just telling Rachel and Sarah about how beautiful Gallopia is, especially our capital city of Ruma." Mark tells us, holding Sarah's hand proudly with a grin. "Maybe you can come to visit after the festival."

"I would love too, but Jacob has us leaving for Polla right after the festival." I respond with a frown at not being able to go to Gallopia.

" Actually, I have my own travel plans in mind." Rachel replies, nibbling at a piece of toast before getting a sickly expression. I'm about to ask but she shakes her head. "I'm a little woozy, nothing to worry about." Nodding, I go back to eating my meal as Rachel starts talking about her plans. "I decided to go visit my mother's family up north." She announces leaving Sarah and I shocked. Rachel has always long to visit her relatives in the north. However troubles at home always got in her way of making the journey.

"What made you finally decide to go." Sarah asks, having similar thoughts as myself.

"You all are leaving. Why not take a chance besides my uncle, who invited me long ago. It's time I meet him in person." Rachel remarks but something about her mannerism is off. I'm about to comment on it when Jacob speaks.

"Maybe instead of going north you should come to Polla with us. "At his suggestion my mood changes at the concept of Rachel being in

Polla. It almost excuses whatever she is hiding if it means I get to stay with my best friend.

"He took my idea" Mark declares in a huff. "I was going to invite you to come with us. "

"Thank you for the offers but I think I'll start in Neva. " Rachel declines politely not meeting our eyes. " I might decide to visit you all a little later in my travels though."

"Why Neva?" I question, feeling suspicious about her plans. Yes I'm disappointed about her refusal but why act cagey about the matter.

"I got something important to discuss with my uncle first" she says, her face saddens. Seeing this I stop my interrogation letting the matter drop. It's obvious Rachel is stressed about something and did not need my prodding.

"That really is a shame Rachel. I would have love for you to come to Gallopia with me" Sarah mumbles in disappointment.

"Me too" she answers, wiggling in her chair repositioning her dress.

"Speaking of the festival Rachel, you look lovely." Sarah praises looking at our friend in awe. I finally take notice of my friend's attire and see Sarah's right. Rachel is wearing a light pink dress with a navy ribbon showing off her small waist. The garb is nicely hemmed to reach my friend's long legs. The dress color was terrific on her dark caramel skin with an amber necklace to match her eyes.

"Gail outdid herself on this one." I already know this dress isn't Rachel's style at all. First my friend hates the color pink and the only person who could get her to wear it is her mother Gail.

"I know right I hate this pink mess of a dress." My tall friend groans, pulling out a hairpin from her hair. "These hairpins are driving me slowly crazy, they keep poking me in the scalp."

"That dress must have cost a small fortune." Sarah examines touching the soft material. "She's serious about getting you married this time." Wincing at Sarah's words, Rachel looks ready to crack, and who can blame her. Recently Rachel's mother has taken a bigger role in her daughter's life after shunning her for five years. Gail only really cares about her three eldest sons ignoring Rachel and her little brother Jordan. And the only reason for the change is she believes Rachel's marriage could elevate the family's name.

"And worst of all, my opinions are being ignored." Rachel cries, surprising everyone with her sudden emotions. " I don't want to be dolled up to try to catch a husband. I already have someone I love deeply."

Patting her back I console her, hating to see my strong friend upset. "What's she saying this time?" I ask knowing this has something to do with Gail.

"That I can't marry Cody because he is white. She even made me wear this pink monstrous dress so wealthy black men will notice me." Rachel sniffs pulling at the dress angrily.

"Rachel, maybe you can hide out here. " Sarah proposes but Rachel frowns at the suggestion.

"It will not work, she has my older brothers spying on me." Rachel sighs and then mutters in a dreamlike state. " I just wish she can see what a good man Cody is despite his skin color.."

Grimacing Sarah and I have the same expression of doubts about Cody's character. Yet the gods must have been smiling on us creating a distraction. "Rachel, you keep saying black men instead of all men." Mark interrupts." Will your mother disapprove of you marrying outside of your race?"

"My mother believes that's the only way our blood can carry on.She will only recognize my marriage if I marry a black man." Rachel admits looking down in shame at her mother's racial bias. .

Everyone stays quiet at her confession until Jacob speaks. "Your mother sounds difficult but even she can't ignore a status higher than commoner. If a man of a different race asks for your hand she has to accept."

My friends and I giggle at the comment knowing how Gail would react. After receiving frosty looks from Mark and Jacob we settled down to explain.. "Rachel's mother is a stubborn woman that never changes her mind. She still blames me for breaking a vase in her home with a ball." I told the guys still laughing a little. "Her oldest son Michael was the one who broke it.. I was not even inside but Gail banned me from her home for two years."

"Fine, your mother is problematic," Jacob relents. "However, even she can't go against the rules of the festival" he argues. "Those rules state that a prince or royal can choose a bride from any culture without the family's refusal ."

"That is true, but my mother will argue an exception." Rachel says removing another hairpin from her hair.

"That is only if the woman is already promised to another man." Mark clarifies covering the main exception written under the law but Gail has an ace up her sleeve.

"That is only one of them. There are plenty of exceptions to the rule including not leaving because of poverty. My mother will claim losing me will be a financial hurdle. " Rachel informs both royals, shocking them with that knowledge.

"She's right, Gail's business uses Rachel's magic to make medicine to support her family." Sarah reveals that fact with a growl. I feel her anger knowing that Gail uses Rachel's gift to make money and doesn't spend a cent to feed her or Jordan with it. Most of the time Rachel has to take on extra work to support Jordan and herself.

"I'm guessing she won't dispute a claim if you marry a black man." Mark scowls figuring out the answer for himself.

"No," She says in a defeated voice." It's too hard dealing with her anymore. I'm hoping leaving after the festival might help matters."

"So that's the true reason for your departure." I answer, understanding Rachel's behavior from earlier.

"Yes, maybe time away from my mother will teach her the error of her ways. Cody even agreed to wait for me and be faithful while I'm away" Rachel responds proudly. I don't know who chokes up first Sarah or me. We both know that's never going to happen. Cody can't be faithful if Rachel is in the next room.

"I don't think you should be going alone," Sarah remarks. "Something might happen, someone should go with you."

"Maybe we can go with you to Neva to make sure you meet your uncle." I offer but a throat clearing makes me look at very unamused green eyes .

"Andy, did you forget about marrying me?" Jacob reminds me in a solemn voice and I have to bite my lip not sound angry.

"Jacob, she cannot go by herself, someone's got to go with her " I argue back. I stare down my fiance waiting for his new statement but someone intervenes.

"Andy, I can go by myself" Rachel disputes. "I've been taking care of myself and Jordan for five years. I think going to Neva will be a piece of cake."

"I agree with Andy," Mark quizzically. "Neva is in questionable leadership, and the once stable country is a lawless state. A single woman shouldn't be traveling alone right now. I wouldn't be resigned to losing Sarah for a short time, to see you safely delivered to your uncle's home".

""Thank you Mark," Sarah says, hugging him.

It's my turn to turn to Jacob waiting for his answer, and I didn't have long to wait. "Fine, you can go "he declares. I squeal, running up to my friends joining them in our happy dance. "I think we made a dumb decision." I hear Jacob mumble but I can care less. I'm going to Neva with my best friends.

"Maybe we can get Laura to go," Sarah suggests, grinning in happiness.

"Good idea this will be the best trip ever." Rachel agrees. " Laura joining the trip would make our little group complete. This trip will be our last adventure together and I can't wait for it to begin."

Games and Relatives

"Now that this is settled lets enjoy the festival," Jacob announces leading our group out of the Inn. When I step outside I can't help but smile at the transformation of the village. Instead of the dull brown buildings and the depressing air of recent raids to our crops. Weston's buildings are wrapped in red and yellow fabrics to symbolize the colors in the Petra flag. There are booths lined along the roads offering games, merchandise, and foods. The people's moods seemed to brighten up with joy as most tried their hands at the games.

Still scanning the area, I spot a game with bottles stacked upon one another and three balls that spark my interest. Smiling, I know I had to try this game out myself. "Hey guys, let's play this game. It seems like fun." I insist, walking to an elderly man that runs the booth.

Seeing me, he gives a kind smile. "Do you want to try your luck?" He asks grinning more when the entire group appears behind me.

"Yes please." I respond eagerly, handing over the money to play the game. The old man scoops up the coins and produces two more balls.

"The goal of this game is to knock over all the bottles and win a prize." The man explains gesturing to the trinkets on the shelves behind him. Seeing something red I instantly know what I want to win.

Squinting my eyes, I toss the first ball knocking over all the bottles on my first try.

"Good aim," the old man cheers . I smile and point towards a red scarf that caught my eye. Grabbing the scarf he hands it to me and I tie it around Jacob's neck.

" I think you look good in red" I compliment making my fiancé blush. "Take a throw, it's fun." I urge Jacob, giving him one of my balls. He glances at the game before shrugging and adjusting his new scarf.

Smiling with his usual cockiness, Jacob waits for the man to stack the bottles again. Once set up he tries to copy my throw from moments ago but fails. His aim was so off he almost hit the booth twenty feet away in the opposite direction of us.

I don't know if it is the awe of the moment or Jacob's red face of embarrassment. Nonetheless laughter fills our group and even the surrounding villagers chuckle a little bit.

"Not all of us have good aim " the old man murmurs at Jacob's retreating form..

Deciding to cheer Jacob up I lean in to give him a kiss on the cheek. "Good try honey." I laugh with Jacob rolling his eyes, turning my peck into a full-blown kiss.

"I might not have won that game, but I'm still getting a prize." He remarks after the kiss earning only a grin from me.

Up next is Rachel who looks ready to play. "Give it all you got Rachel" I cheer on my friend.

"I'll do my best" she laughs but quickly frowns at the man in the booth.. Trying to understand my friend's sour expression I quickly realize the man is gawking at her chest.

"If I was forty years younger." The man grins slyly, getting Rachel angrier and the rest of our group joins her.

"Sir, can you please give her the balls and reframe from leering at our friend's breasts." Jacob demands and the harshness of the words snaps the man out of his daze. In an instant, Rachel has three balls in her hand. After that she did win a prize on her second throw. A beaded necklace is what she chose and Mark decides to give it a try. Similar to myself he won on the first shot giving Sarah a stuffed animal.

"Let's try another game," Mark declares, scanning the other booths around us. Nodding in agreement we move to another game until a voice calling Jacob's name catches our notice. A blond-haired boy that looks to be sixteen comes running up to us with two other boys.

"Travis, what are you doing here?" Jacob bellows happily giving the blond boy a giant hug. The hug is affectionate and that name makes me remember something my fiancé told me.

"Jacob, Travis is the name of your youngest brother. Is this him by chance?" I interrupt the two being reminded of the conversation we had about his three brothers and mother. Analyzing the two I can see a resemblance in their faces and eye color. Although Travis is fairer than Jacob with lighter hair and complexion..

"Yes, I am Jacob's youngest brother" Travis answers and then points to the other two boys next to him." These are my friends James Harris and David Morris." Introducing a black youth and a skinny boy with huge glasses with shy smiles on their faces.

"Nice to meet you, I'm Andy Miller. And these are my friends Sarah Palmer, and Rachel Goodman." Trying to act calm but inside I'm freaking out. I can't believe I'm meeting one of my in-laws right now.

"It's my pleasure to meet you all" Travis flirts winking at me.

At that Jacob's demeanor changes wrapping his arms around my waist possessively.. "Travis Andy is my future bride. So please keep your flirting to yourself" he commands angrily.

At that declaration Travis didn't look shocked but extremely joyous ripping me out of his brother's hands. "That's excellent, finally I have a sister." He gushes, swinging me around so many times I get a little dizzy. I'm glad when Jacob breaks us apart so I can get my bearings back. Observing Travis he seems to be a good boy with a giddy personality as his focus turns to Mark.

"Travis, it is very nice to see you again and like Jacob, I have good news too." Mark says taking Sarah's hand showing the relationship to the young royal. Beaming Travis greets the other prince with the same earnest smile.

"What a beauty you found." Travis says bluntly inspecting Sarah's red dress which makes her bust huge. Blushing realizing what the young royal's eyes are fixating on. Sarah tries to cover up, but it just makes it worse.

A smack on the side of Travis's head quickly ends the shameful gawking. "Travis, you are being a pervert and should apologize to my Sarah" Mark scolds the younger noble.

"But she has nice breasts" Travis whines and earns another smack on the back of his head. After that Mark starts lecturing Travis on etiquette. Watching this I can tell this will be a long conversation and I decide to focus my attention on the other boys.

"James, it's been a long time. How is your family?" Jacob asks the black youth that looks to be fifteen. However he is six feet tall with a slender muscular body. Although something about the boy seems familiar, especially his amber eyes and dark caramel skin. It is bugging me as I continue listening to their conversation.

"They're fine" James says but his attention is on Rachel now. He looks like he saw a ghost when she comes near. My friend also looks puzzled staring at his face.

"James, do you know a man by the name of Randal Harris." Rachel questions but it seems she already knows the answer.

"Yes, that's my father," James immediately answers. And that's when Rachel squeals in joy and I can't get why but Sarah did.

"Rachel, that's your uncle's name right," Sarah says and the pieces begin to fit in my head. Now I know why James' features look so familiar. Staring at Rachel and James the two could pass as siblings with their height and features so closely matching.

"Yes, he's the one I am visiting." Rachel begins but her words are interrupted by a screaming child. The child in question rushes full speed jumping at her body. Almost instinctively, she catches the boy and puts him on the ground.

"Stop doing that Jordan" Rachel fusses at the boy with a stern face. Grinning with two-front teeth missing, Jordan just squeezes his sister harder as a response. Still filled with energy, he loses interest in Rachel and comes scrambling to me.

Knowing it was better to get to Jordan's eye level. I'm ready when he flings his long legs around my waist. "Andy, look I lost another tooth" he hollers at the top of his lungs showing me his missing teeth.

"I see, soon you'll be toothless and can't eat anymore candy." I tease the little boy who pouts revealing an adorable face.

"No! That cannot happen, I love candy" Jordan stomps stubbornly at my ribbing.

"She is pulling your leg Jordan," Rachel says, giving me that look that means tell the truth or else. Knowing my fun was over I rub his head playfully.

"She's right, I was just joking. There is plenty of candy you can eat with that mouth of yours." And with that Jordan is back to his usual self. I turn to Rachel to find her looking at Jordan and James in amazement. Minus the chubby cheeks of the seven-year-old they both have the same face. James could pass as Jordan's older brother.

"That's why you're asking about your uncle, because of the likeness." I confirm realizing Rachel would catch the resemblance better than any of us. Nodding she smiles before swinging her arms around James to hug him. The poor boy looks stunned but accepts the hug with such eagerness.

"Hello, cousin I guess we have some introductions to do." Rachel happily letting go of the boy and pointing to Jordan talking to Jacob about his new shoes. "The kid that hasn't stopped talking since he got here is my little brother Jordan. And as Andy said, I am Rachel, your long lost cousin."

James is about to speak when his friend shakes his shoulder forcefully. "What is the matter, David?" He asks the boy with the glasses who hadn't uttered a word since we met.

"James this kid could be your brother" David stumbles out looking at Jordan.

"We are cousins David, it would make sense there would be similarities." He says waving off his friend's surprise expression and returning his focus on Rachel again. "My father has been trying to get in touch with you for years. We never got a response back from you, why is that.."

"That wasn't my fault mother burns your father's letters for some reason." Rachel says in defense of herself.

"That's horrible but it's nice to know you weren't ignoring us on purpose. " James mumbles brushing off Gail burning his father's letters. "·I guess it would be too much to ask to meet Aunt Gail."

"That isn't a good idea, " Rachel warns. "My mother isn't a very pleasant woman to be around, period. I would advise you to avoid meeting her or my other brothers while you're staying in Weston."

"Fine, I guess I will never know why she burnt father's letters."

"It doesn't matter anymore what my mother wants. I plan to go visit your father after the festival ends anyway."

"Really!"

"Yes my friends and I are going " Rachel affirms and James looks ready to burst.

"Then, let me escort you to Malloria." He offers, missing the look of shock on Rachel's face and ours. Malloria is a whole different kingdom than what we thought his family lived in.

"I thought you lived in Neva" Sarah interrupts.

"We do when my father is doing his diplomatic duties. However he is a Duke in Malloria and that is where he is most of the time." James corrected us.

Rachel gets over her shock fast and laughs. "I guess it's good we ran into you or we would have been going to the wrong kingdom." And with that the two cousins discuss travel plans for the trip. I'm listening to the two when Jacob wraps his arms around my waist.

"Andy, since James offered to escort Rachel to Malloria. You can come with me to Polla now" He says smiling like he won a prize.

"No way, I'm still going." I vow sticking my tongue out but our banter is interrupted by someone pulling on the hem of my dress. Looking down I can see brown eyes that are filled with tears.

"Andy, are you really leaving?" Jordan asks with tears in his eyes.

My heart is breaking at the question by the little boy I thought of as a brother. I practically spent most of Jordan's life as a part time caretaker helping Rachel raise the boy. Tears fill my own eyes as I reach to hug the child and comfort him, but Jacob speaks first.

"Yes, she is but you can visit when Rachel comes back from her journey.." Instantly I knew he said the wrong thing as the distress increased on Jordan's face. Yelling in my head my fiancé is an idiot. I see the plants around the boy growing rapidly. . Oh crap Jordan accidently activated his magic and I get a bad feeling things are about to get worse.

"Sissy can't go," Jordan yells as a light glow appears around him. After that the mayhem starts as tree roots shot out of the earth destroying stalls and panicking the masses. People scream and move away from the boy losing control of his magic the more he weeps. . Dropping to his eye level hoping to calm the little wizard down. "Jordan, you have to stay calm."

My words didn't seem to be getting through to Jordan as his magic conjures something up more dangerous. The only warning is a thick wall of dust rising in the air and the howling winds. "It's a dust storm" a random woman screeches as the storm picks up with increasing speed. The yells are deafening as people swarm for shelter as dust gets into their eyes and nose making it hard to breathe. Getting bump into I try to shield Jordan, as people are hitting us from all directions. "Andy, " Jacob shouts, reaching for my right hand pulling Jordan and myself into the corner between the stands. The little niche is just roomy enough to fit the three of us, saving us from the suffocating dust.

"Where are the others?" I wheeze out, wiping my eyes trying to see my friends. "I cannot see them."

"I think they went for shelter, but we need to stop this. It's getting dangerous" Jacob yells pointing at the chaos everywhere around us. Looking around, I knew if we didn't halt the storm someone would get hurt or worse.

"It's alright Jacob. Jordan can stop the storm because he's a big boy." I reply smiling at the bright child who looks scared and panicked.

"I cannot make it stop" Jordan weeps his panic creating a mighty gale that knocks over food stands around us. Swallowing nervously, I pull him into my lap trying to comfort the boy.

"Jordan, close your eyes and focus on getting control over your magic." I instructed rubbing the child's back in a soothing motion trying to relieve his nerves. I recognize his fear is what's causing the trouble so I need to erase it.. Humming a tune that Jordan loves, I feel his muscles relax. He starts to wipe his eyes and the tears stop flowing. Once the little boy is soothed the storm ends. I look up to see the sun is out and everything is back to normal.

"Jordan, good job" I praise hugging the child grateful that the dust storm is over. Although trouble is coming our way in the form of three angry men with scowls written on their faces. Pushing Jordan behind me, I wait for the confrontation that is about to happen.

Wizard Revealed

"It's the Goodman boy." Tim points out one of the three men standing in front of me glaring at Jordan behind me." He is the cause of that freak storm." The older Walker roars to the people, getting many of them to yell at Jordan.

I can feel Jordan trembling and I try my best to protect him."Mr. Walker he's a child and the storm was an accident. He didn't mean anyone any harm." I state in defense of Jordan but mockery is all I get for my efforts.

"An accident is breaking mommy's vase not causing a dust storm." Tim announces with many other people in the village in agreement. " I think the boy needs to be punished for the chaos he caused."

"He needs to be run out of the village." Cody Walker proposes with Matthew nodding along with his brother. Feeling my stomach drop as I see a surge come from the crowd with people yelling their support. Fear races over me but mostly anger at people I thought I knew turning into monsters.

"Cody, your family does not know anything about magic. So, shut your mouth and stop threatening Jordan." I remark glaring at the men daring them to take a step closer. "He is a child and the only wizard to be born in this village, not a criminal."

"Andy's right, leave the boy alone. " One lady screams in agreement and I can't help but be proud. At least some people haven't lost their minds.

"You should be on our side, Andy. You're my brother's fiancée," Cody alleges looking at Matthew who now was quiet and sullen.

"She isn't his fiancée but mine." Jacob hisses glaring at Matthew and his family standing beside me. I feel happy to have Jacob's aid. His status alone should help, and I can see Tim losing his bravado.

Looking more gracious Tim gives a smile to Jacob. "Your Highness, it is good to see you again. Congratulations to you and Andy I understand." If Matthew looked disturbed before he is really bothered now at his father's chumminess with Jacob.

"I'd say the same but what just happened here left a bad taste in my mouth." Jacob declares frowning at the Walkers, but Tim missed the hint entirely.

"I'm sorry for any trouble this menace caused you." Tim says starting to go around me to get to Jordan. Just as Tim reaches for Jordan with his hand I slap it away.

"He isn't a menace, but a wizard learning his powers." I shout and for Tim's part he looks pissed at me for hitting his hand. However Tim takes one glance at Jacob and chooses wisely to swallow what he wanted to say.

"He is a demon." Matthew argues looking at Jordan with hate that would make anyone tremble.

"He is a boy with great powers and I agree with my fiancée," Jacob replies, putting a gentle hand around me. Moving us further into the corner Jacob unsheathed his sword. "I will not let harm come to him." His announcement makes Tim angry enough to speak.

"This is none of your concern," Tim yells, his façade long gone. "You are just visiting and hold no bearing on any decision we make with the boy." Reaching past me again, Tim is blocked immediately.

"I cannot sit back and watch a child get bullied by grown men." Jacob declares firmly pushing the man away. Huffing Tim is surprised by the action and stands still unsure what to do.

"I am banishing that demon from Weston even if I have to beat this royal to do so." Matthew shouts lunging forward but a disturbance in the crowd stops his attempts. Shoving and pushing people Rachel comes sprinting out of the crowd.

"Matthew, if you touch my brother, I'll bury you alive" She threatens our friends at her back. Moving to form a circle around us, our friends face the crowd. Rachel takes up a spot between Matthew and me glaring at the Walkers. Although her eyes became bigger seeing Cody with the ones leading the charge.

"Cody, what are you doing? " She asks in a shaken voice.

"Getting rid of the trash," Cody states proudly with a couple men in the crowd cheering him on. Hearing that Rachel's face is stricken. I didn't think it was just the crowd that put my friend in a sullen mood.

"My brother has done nothing wrong, just lost control of his magic. It happens to beginners" Rachel tries to clarify, but her plea fails to convince Cody otherwise.

"He's a freak of nature that shouldn't have been born in this world." Cody bellows out. The harshness of the words hit us all, but Rachel is most affected.

"How can you say that Cody? Jordan is a gift." She responds, reaching out her hand for her love to understand. "There are only a handful of men with magic. He's special."

"Yes, that's exactly right," Cody cackles, throwing her words back at her. "Women are meant to have magic, not men. He's abnormal and I for one don't want Jordan in my village. We should drop the little freak outside the village and let the wolves have him." I see the rage immediately in Rachel's face and I'm happy she's finally seeing the truth about Cody.

"I will not let you do that." Rachel yells all her feelings of betrayal gone as her fists are out. "If anyone comes near him they will have to get through me first." Showing she meant business, her eyes began to glow. Looking at my friend I knew if push comes to shove, people will get hurt if they lay one finger on Jordan. Rachel is in mama mode, and Cody's charm isn't going to get him out of this mess.

"Rachel, your brother isn't like you and should be set free like an animal." Cody starts but that flash of hurt that crosses Rachel's face is the only warning. She shoves him to the ground with tears in her eyes.

"If you even try it, you will regret it" She warns her eyes glowing.

"Rachel, listen to reason and understand that your brother isn't beneficial to the village." Cody continues not the least bit worried by Rachel's threat. I want badly to go over and slap the man for his words but reframed. Leaving would leave Jordan unprotected, and Rachel has to do this on her own.

"Cody, my brother isn't a tool for this village." Rachel roars and she did something I didn't predict. Her hand flies over Cody's face, slapping his cheek.

Touching his face, I can see Cody's whole demeanor change. "Rachel, you are fighting a losing battle so stop before you cause trouble for yourself."

"My brother is my everything. I will always stick by him.You on the other hand are replaceable,we are done." I silently cheer inside at hearing those words from Rachel's mouth but feel sorry it takes this for her to end the courtship. And the way Cody is taking it he wasn't happy.

"Rachel, calm down and think of what you are giving up for that piece of trash." He presses demeaning Jordan further and my best friend gets livid.

"My brother isn't trash, and I am finally thinking clearly for once. I should've listen to my friends when they said you were no good."

"You're not leaving me" he hisses, grabbing her arm.

"Let go of me" Rachel wincing in pain.

"No, you are mine and always will be," Cody says in a possessive voice.

"Hey, let her go now." I yell, coming to Rachel's defense, but a large man appears suddenly. Removing Cody's hand from Rachel and practically throwing him into Matthew with such ease.

Shocked, Cody is now on the ground gawking at the man with fear, and I can't blame him. The man has to be seven feet tall and the menacing look he's giving Cody is frightening. His face alone can make a child run home to his mama. A long scar covering his pale face and wild auburn locks made him look almost feral.

"Don't touch the girl" he barks at Cody waiting for a reaction. Cody looks downright petrified as he pulls himself off the ground. Instead of challenging the giant he moves his focus elsewhere.

"Thanks," Rachel says, looking at her savior with hesitation.

"No problem." The giant grunts out before looking around the crowd. "It looked like you needed help, pretty girl." That last part makes me groan. Why did this man have to say that?

Rachel's face scrunches up instantly at the comment. "I was handling it."

Snorting he replies, "Sure being manhandled was obviously part of your plan." The man looks down smirking at Rachel. "I see you have a lot of pride, but next time pick a better love interest."

"Why, you imbecile." She insulted looking ready to rant, but I had enough. They're both acting ridiculous and forgetting about the angry crowd around us.

"Rachel, focus" I shout and I'm not the only one thinking the same thing.

"Sir, we're in the middle of something as you can see." Jacob points out still looking at the crowd with seriousness. The man sees what Jacob is referring to and merely grins.

"Well, let me help you. I haven't had a good fight in a long time." Pulling out what looked to be the broadest long sword that I ever saw under his cloak. The blade is almost Jordan's height and probably weighed more than the child himself. "Oh, and my name is Malcolm, not sir. It makes me sound old and I'm about the same age as you."

. "Seriously you look like you're in your thirties" Rachel remarks.

"Hey honey I am only twenty-six, don't put me in that age range yet".

"Don't call me honey." She screeches, throwing a fit. And with that the two begin an argument which sounds more like a lover's quarrel.

"Oh, is this why you're throwing me away? For this brute" Cody accuses.

Rachel's fury is now back on Cody at his remark. "No, I am leaving you for insulting and threatening my brother." She says each word slowly so he can understand them. "I don't want to be with you anymore." The finality of her words seems to get to Cody.

"Rachel, you don't mean that right" he pleads.

He's about to speak again but his father silenced him "Cody stop son you can do so much better than her." Tim states in an arrogant tone.

"Yes brother it's better this way. You're spared from joining a family that makes monsters like Jordan. "Matthew declares, spitting out these words.

"Don't talk about my family." Rachel yells.

"Maybe your brother isn't the only one that's messed up in the head Rachel. " Matthew taunts. A few people in the crowd join him making pointing motions towards the siblings. Rachel only stays still as her whole body lit up with magic flowing into the ground where Matthew is standing. The dirt and rocks in that area start to dissolve until there's nothing left but quicksand. The youngest Walker begins to sink as his family watches in horror.

Panicking, Matthew begs for help from his father and brother. However neither lifted a finger to aid him both scared to move. Seeing Matthew shoulder deep in the sand I must admit Rachel is getting a little out of hand.

"Rachel, I think that is enough." I shout getting no response from my friend and Mathew is now submerged to his neck in sand. "Rachel stop, your point is proven." Grabbing my friend's shoulders, shaking her hard.

Snapping out of her anger Rachel sighs but relents. "Fine" she mumbles, transforming the sand into dirt again. Luckily Matthew's head is still visible or else Rachel would be in a lot of trouble. "I wasn't going to kill him but making good on my threat." She explains turning back to the screaming head." Remember Matthew, I told you I was going to bury you if you said anything about my family."

The villagers only chuckle at her response and the comedy of Matthew's situation. Tim finally finds his voice looking at the crowd for support as he speaks. "Look at what she tried to do to my son. She almost killed him.."

I knew most villagers didn't like the Walkers. However, they kept their opinions silent because Tim was known to be vindictive. Seeing Rachel stand up against him must have given them courage because many made their feelings known. Many hoots and curses at the Walkers not feeling sorry for Matthew.

"I want this girl arrested" Tim rants getting furious at the people's reaction to his family.

"Be quiet, you're causing a scene." An unknown man, orders who don't seem much older than me.

"What did you say to me boy?" Tim challenges the new comer.

"I want you to leave the girl alone and don't press charges against her." The stranger announces with an authority in his voice that made any lesser man shrink. Although Tim didn't falter, going so far as to snap back.

"Why are you even getting involved in this matter? What reason would I not press charges against this girl" Tim asks ?

The stranger just lifts his brows at Tim's bluntness. "Okay, I'll explain it to you old man." The stranger announces his blue eyes getting sharper as Tim gasps at being called old. "Your son and the entire family were threatening harm to the child. It's in his sister's right to defend him to the best of her ability." The stranger's words are simple but hold merit.

"She was going to kill him" Tim accuses as the stranger just laughs.

"Your son was never in real danger. I can see the girl wasn't going to really harm him." The man gives Rachel a wink and Tim a hard stare." She isn't as heartless as your family. And as for who I am, let me introduce myself." With that, the man spun around and did a swooping bow. "I'm your sovereign, King Louis of Perta." At that, I think everyone in the crowd gasps and Tim looks ready to faint.

The King of Perta

There in front of us stands King Louis of Perta looking like any ordinary villager. Wearing a simple blue shirt with black pants that any common man would possess. He looks to be at least six feet three and very handsome, smiling at the crowd. His long black hair is tied in a loose ponytail and well-tanned face is at least neatly shaved.

"What is he doing here? " Sarah whispers in awe.

"I don't know, but he's on our side so let's be thankful." I respond happily at how things are turning out.

Tim on the other hand lost all his previous bravado and seemed petrified by the turn of events.. Dropping to his knees and placing his head on the ground. "I sincerely apologize for my outburst, my King. " He proclaims quickly to the king before continuing. " It has been a stressful experience due to that girl's demon of a brother and the chaos he created."

"My brother isn't a demon but an earth wizard" Rachel refutes before gazing at the king dropping on her knees also. "Jordan never hurt anyone with his power and the dust storm isn't the norm for him, your Majesty." She explains her voice taking a respectful tone when speaking to the king. "He's a good boy and at only seven it takes time to learn magic especially for a young child."

"I can understand that" King Louis comments, giving Rachel a gentle smile. " Luckily your brother didn't cause that much damage. And that's why I recommend we call this matter all forgotten and enjoy the festival." Raising his voice he announces to all the crowd. "My people the boy is just a child and should be afforded leniency, do you not agree?"

Cheers joined the King's announcement, and I breathed a sigh of relief.

"Your majesty I must strongly interject on this matter" Tim counters furiously. "Just because the child hasn't caused anyone harm today. Doesn't mean he cannot in the future." Pointing his finger at the siblings, glaring at them. "These siblings are a danger to us good citizens and should be killed on the spot."

Outrage is the immediate reaction in all of our faces as we all surround Rachel and Jordan in protection. Our group of friends create a shield blocking the now stun siblings from the raving Tim and his madness. Killing them wasn't even a possibility under the law and everyone knows it.

"Arrest them King Louis, and cut off their heads!" Tim adds his eyes bulging and spitting out the words waiting for the king to do his bidding. Instead King Louis only sneers in displeasure at Tim's action looking highly irate.

"Sir, what is your name?" The King orders stiffly glaring at Tim.

Missing the glare Tim smirks at us like he won. "I am Tim Walker." And with a gesture he points to where Cody is unsuccessfully trying to unearth his brother." And these are my sons Matthew and Cody."

"Okay Tim, I recommend staying out of my affairs and never questioning my judgment again." King Louis dictates astounding Tim and his sons finally realizing things aren't going their way. "And furthermore leave the girl and her brother alone before you are the ones arrested." At that threat the king turns to leave but Tim seizes his arm stopping him.

" You cannot do this, we are the victims" Tim yells, almost shaking King Louis. I'm shocked that Tim would be so bold to do such a thing. To grab a member of a noble family without permission is a grave error and Tim just committed it in front of hundreds of people.

"I think you should let go, before my men assist you." King Louis commands as two huge soldiers surround Tim in a matter of seconds.

Realizing his mistake Tim let go of the King's arm, but he still looks defiant. "Why your Highness, this boy is nothing but a freak."

Turning around the King's face turns to stone . "I have always hated people who think they are above others. And if you continue with this harassment. I will decree half of your wealth be given to the boy. Do you understand " The announcement floored Tim into silence.

"Is it wrong that I am hoping that Tim continues to harass Jordan?" Rachel says quietly to me and with that I give my friend a glare. " Hey, that money could go a long way for Jordan and myself in the future." She mutters as our focus returns to Tim and the king.

"Your Highness, this isn't fair, I'm a wealthy trader and land mapper in the west." Tim gripes throwing a tantrum like a child. "That boy is a demon and should be treated as such." He adds to offending Jordan again but this time the king takes Tim's words into consideration.

Seeing this change I hope that Tim's reputation will not sway the King's actions. Although my worries aren't founded as King Louis signals all his guards to come forward. There were so many of them and some are wearing plain clothes, blending in with the crowd. Swords are drawn and all these men's attention is on Tim.

"This is getting interesting." Malcolm laughs, enjoying the drama that was unfolding before us.

"That, we agree on" Mark answers laughing along with the red haired giant. Shaking my head somehow I became the sane one of my friends as I observe what is happening with Tim with calmness.

" Good I thought we have to look for you for days. Nonetheless fate delivered you straight to us on the first day. " King Louis says when two of his guards restrain Tim placing him on his knees..

"Why are you doing this, your highness?" Tim contends struggling against his capturers. At that question I wanted an answer also of why the king was looking for Tim.

"Are you Mason Walker the trader of the Macron Mountain?" The King challenge looking like he already knew the answer.

"Yes, Mason is my first name" Tim answers honestly.

"Then there is no mistake. You, Mason T. Walker is charged with treason against Perta" King Louis declares startling everyone around us in horror. Mouths are open at this new turn of events that many of the villagers stagger back a little.

"I would never do such a thing." Tim contested denying the claim against him but he seems nervous to me. The sweat coming from his brows and his body language is twitchy, something isn't quite right there.

"Mason Walker, you and your sons are accused of being the cause of Weston's troubles." King Louis rebuffs with his own allegation as his guards come to arrest Cody next. Placing him beside his father to stand and face the king's claims. "Your family is the reason for all the deaths in Weston because of your dealings with the Delianians."

At that the declaration is met with disbelief and a little rage. Everyone listening cannot believe what they are hearing. Can it be true that the Walkers have been working with the raiders for a year now.

"My King, you must be mistaken" Tim argues. "There must be another man by that name because I would never work with those vile people."

"We have proof of your guilt and plenty of witnesses." The King announces and Tim's face turns white in fear and all doubts are gone from my mind. "They witnessed all your dealings with the invaders and we arrested the guardsman that let the Delianians escape from Weston."

Murmurs around us grow louder and someone finally speaks up. "What is this business about the guards and how does the crown know of our affairs?"

"Yes, how do we know it's true? The crown abandoned us when we needed help the most." One angry woman shouts who lost a son in one of the raids. "My son died when you didn't read our letters." Falling apart the woman's husband consoles her and seeing that, the king has a saddened expression.

"Sorry for the loss my dear woman." King Louis says earnestly. " And to answer your question the crown did not respond to your village letters . It's because Mason Walker didn't send them."

"How can that be possible if we sent dozens of letters for a year? You are telling me that you didn't even get one?" I ask looking at the king's face and he nods in confirmation..

"Sadly, none of the letters got to my advisors or me. The only reason we know of the raids is that a former villager who left came to the capital. After that, I sent spies to uncover the troubles in the west." King Louis explains his investigation and directs an accusing finger towards the Walkers. "And my people found you are the cause of everything."

"Sir, how are they guilty?" Rachel questions looking at Cody and his father in disgust.

"Well my dear, did you ever wonder why every obstacle or defense you put up never seemed to stop the Delianians?" King Louis asked the whole crowd."You doubled up on men and created walls, but the Delianians kept sneaking in."

"What do you mean by all this? " One man yells after losing his patience.

"He is saying that someone has been leaking your secrets to the enemies." Malcolm declares before gesturing to the Walkers. "And I am guessing these gentlemen are the prime suspects or he just likes looking at them because they are pretty."

Laughing at the comment King Louis answers. "they certainly are not." Yet the good humor was gone when he got back to the Walkers. "You let the enemy raid Weston without mercy. For the money and the promise of riches." Tim was trying to speak, but the King wouldn't hear it. "Don't deny it, your underlings turned on you when they were caught." King Louis motions for two men to be brought forward. Looking at both men, I recognized them instantly. Both men aren't what most would call decent people and would probably sell their own mother for a few coins. "We found these two men with a known

Delianians spy. And after a lot of talking and persuasion. These men are willing to testify to save their lives."

"I can explain, I was only doing that to help Weston," Tim professed in a nervous voice." They said if we aided them people would not come to harm. They lied to me."

"Really" the King quips. "If that were true, what is this that we found in a shipment these two geniuses were bringing to you." And with an order a big trunk was brought forth. When it is opened the villagers are speechless. Thousands of coins and gems filled the chest and the Walkers' guilt is undeniable now. Seeing the proof Tim hung his head in defeat. "The riches you acquired will be given to the victims of your greed. Your family will be sent to Helena, the capital, to await trial." With the charges read to them they were put into shackles. Two other guards are too busy digging Matthew out to put him in chains with his brother and father.

When the men finally get Matthew free. The youngest Walker shouts something damning at his father. "Father, you said we wouldn't be caught."

"Be quiet you fool" Tim growls trying desperately to silence his son. Matthew stares at his father in hate and spite.

"I'm going to confess to all your crimes and get mercy, father." He proclaims before switching his gaze to the King. "I will tell you everything, please don't charge me. I know everything my father did and more." He bargains looking at the King waiting for an answer.

The King's response is calculated showing interest in his cooperation. "That can be arranged if your information is good."

"It is, I can guarantee it." Matthew says with a smile. It made me sick to think he might get away with this by cooperating with the King.

"You'd turn on your own family Matthew?" Tim is appalled looking at his son with betrayal in his eyes and I nearly laugh. Did Tim really expect loyalty when one was facing the crime of treason?

"Yes, if it means I can go free and keep my reputation" Matthew replies honestly.. Hearing those words, a familiar feeling comes over me and I know my sight wanted to show me something. Without a second to spare, I grab Rachel's arm. She takes one glance at me and understands moving behind me as my body stiffens up. Images cloud my eyesight of all different things but one clear one is coming into focus. I see two people I think I recognize but they are much older and look completely different. In the vision I see *Mel and Matthew in a tiny hut in what looks to be in the middle of nowhere. Their once perfect appearances are gone with Matthew sporting an ugly scar disfiguring his once handsome face. Mel didn't have any scars thankfully but she was caked in mud and her long blond curls were chopped off.*

"This is your fault." an older Mel screams as I overheard their conversation.

"How is that?" Matthew yells back glaring at Mel looking ready to snap.

"If you didn't get caught with your father that day. Our whole lives could have been different, you buffoon." Mel claims to be throwing what looks to be a rusted pot. Ducking, Matthew barely missed it hitting his head.

Enraged Matthew grabs Mel by the hair pulling her to him. "Let me remind you Melissa," he hisses. "We all made choices in Weston that day." At that ominous remark he throws my sister on the dirty floor like she's a piece of trash." Tears burn my eyes as I witness my sister being abused. This cannot be her fate no one deserves this treatment but as I ponder this thought the vision begins to change.

Another image appears this time of two adorable children a boy, and girl with blond curls. They looked to be around four or five in a building that was filled with children playing. Around them little ones played with dolls and toy soldiers. However the two blonds stayed in their corner looking sad and left out. "David, why do they not like us?" Ask the girl with tears rolling down her face.

"Because we carry the name of bad people." The little boy answers honestly, hugging his sister trying to comfort her.

"We didn't do anything," the girl cries.

"I know that and one day everyone will realize the same." David vows to pat his sister's head. "The Walker name was once respected and we'll make it so again. In the future our parent's sins will not be held against us sister." And with that heartbreaking promise my magic starts to fade and the feeling of awareness comes back to me.

Blinking, I feel strong hands hold me up and Rachel's face appears in my sight line. "Are you back to normal or do I need to slap you?" She questions raising her hand to hit me but I shrug out of her grip.

"Please keep your hands to yourself" I mumbles, still a little dazed.

"So, what did you see? Don't keep me waiting" she probes for information..

Sighing I gesture to Matthew knowing Rachel wouldn't let it go until I told her something. "Matthew, even if he escapes prosecution he will always be viewed as a traitor. People will know him as a criminal. His children are going to be shunned for the mistakes of their parents. The Walker name will never be known in excellence again but will be notorious." I end on that note not wanting to tell Rachel how Mel is tied to this future as well.

Snorting Rachel can't be happier. "It couldn't have happened to a better person." She rejoices in missing my sad expression.

"Yeah" I mumble, not really thinking about Matthew, but those two cute children. Their lives will be ruined just because of the mistakes of their father. And furthermore my sister who is a brat most of the time shouldn't be forced to marry an abuser. Undoubtedly I will stop this union from occurring even if I need to go against fate.

"Let go of me" Cody yells interrupting my inner dialogue. Looking at the idiot struggling in vain with ten guards I can see that Walker's downfall has begun as he pleads for anyone to aid him. Scanning the crowd, his eyes land on his ex-girlfriend. "Rachel, please don't let them take me. Remember you love me. "

Rachel at his begging only turns her back on him ."I wouldn't help you if you were on your last breath." She answers ignoring his cries for help as the soldiers finally drag him away with his father. In chains both men are taken away as the people around them scowl.

"Rachel, are you okay? "I ask her as she didn't shed a tear at Cody being taken away.

"Yes, I'm peachy can't you tell" she says in a sarcastic voice. "I'm just happy this happened before I got engaged to him. Could you imagine being married to a traitor?"

"No, I can't imagine that very thing." I admit speaking more to myself than Rachel. After that we absorbed all this information around us. It seems Matthew's bargain is still being worked on as soldiers led him away like his brother and father.. Although he went without being dragged or the use of chains keeping some dignity. After that Rachel is the only one that remembers her manners as she curtsy for King Louis . Realizing what was happening I did the same and soon our whole group showed our respect to King Louis.

"Your Highness, I want to thank you for your help earlier." Rachel declares pushing Jordan forward as he meekly says thank you as well.

"The honor was all mine and besides meeting a wizard is rare." King Louis says in a gentle voice. The King rubs Jordan's head producing a hard candy earning a smile from the boy.

" Yes, my brother is an oddity making some people feel he's abnormal." Rachel mentions producing a frown at the thought.

"Well, the Walkers will be one less obstacle in his way" the King reassures.

Just when Rachel is about to speak again a giant form appears by her side. "I heard wizards are powerful magic users and that storm proved that fact." Malcolm chuckles picking up Jordan making the boy laugh as he spun him around.

"Please be careful." Rachel warns looking ready to snatch Jordan away when Malcolm turns him upside down.

"Calm down he likes it" Malcolm asserts with Jordan giggling in agreement.

"Fine, but if you drop him. I am going to repeat my performance with Matthew on you."

"Noted" The giant replies by throwing Jordan in the air and catching the child. At that moment I swear Rachel looks ready to throw a punch if Travis's loud voice didn't get everyone's attention.

"James, you have a wizard in your family." Travis congratulated his friend like Jordan was a rare possession to brag about. James ignores the remark walking up to Rachel and Jordan to speak to them.

"Is he always able to make dust storms like that?"

"Yes, but usually things don't get this out of control" Rachel mutters.

"Rachel what other things can Jordan accomplish with magic?" David interjects making Rachel jump as she realizes he is standing right next to her. David who is keeping a keen eye on Jordan like he is a new species writing things in a brown leather journal.

"Nothing different than my own magic, I guess. I make him move rocks and practice growing plants " she replies looking at the boy taking notes.

Nodding, the boy seems to be taking everything in spades. "Rachel wizards and witches are similar but they are actually completely different magic users. Maybe another method could help you with his training." David advises looking at Jordan and frowning. "His magic comes from the earth like yours, but he might have special strengths."

"How do you know so much about magic users?" Rachel inquires, raising her eyebrow at the boy. " Are you a wizard too?"

" I wish but I'm just normal" David responds with a sigh. " My mother is the head witch of Polla so I learnt everything about magic from a young age. It's an interesting subject because every magic user is different in their own way." And with that David came to life and spoke to Rachel about his ideas about Jordan's specialty. I look at the boy with a new light. David's appearance of a slim built boy of fourteen years with grayish eyes that shone through his thick glasses. I assume he was a bookish sort of boy and it seems I was correct in that aspect. However shy he was not, as he is giving Rachel notes about what could help Jordan in his training.

Smiling at that discussion I turn my focus on James chatting with Malcolm like an old friend. "Do you know each other?" I ask the two.

"Yes, Malcolm is the King of Malloria's nephew and his general." James' answer shocks me and my friends completely. I assumed Malcolm was a soldier or just another traveler who came to enjoy the festival, not another royal.

"Malcolm of Malloria, I've heard great things about you," Mark interrupts overhearing James' introduction. "The great warrior who led the battle of Falcon Ridge against the Bulkans killing hundreds of those scoundrels."

At that, my mouth dropped. The Battle of Falcon Ridge is well known, even in Petra. Falcon Ridge is a small militia outpost in Malloria that the Bulkans wanted. The Bulkans are people from the east whose land is barren. And because of that they raid and pilfer other lands around them, and the outpost was one of them. It was a deadly battle won by Malloria due to a young and masterful general Malcolm of Malloria.

"That was me but I got lucky on that." Malcolm contends looking uncomfortable talking about his victory which was brilliantly executed. We all began to swarm him and the men seemed to be star struck around him.

"Luck didn't have anything to do with it." King Louis alleges making his presence known. "It was one of the best strategies formed in battle in more than a decade."

"Well, you're killing my humble vibe here." Malcolm huffs making Mark and King Louis chuckle. "Let's get these introductions out of the way. I am Malcolm of Malloria, the famed general of Falcon Ridge."

"I' m King Jacob of Polla and this is my fiancée Andrea Miller. The blond boy who hasn't stopped talking is my brother Prince Travis." Jacob bowing after making our introductions.

Stepping forward Rachel curtsies."I cannot be rude and since you both saved me, I owe you. I'm Rachel Goodman and this is my brother Jordan." Pointing out James "Our cousin James Harris and his friend David Morris."

"I am Prince Mark of Gallopia, and this is my bride, Sarah Palmer." Mark says ending our introductions.

"I'm happy to meet you all." King Louis greeted politely, looking pleased as he and the men began talking again about Falcon Ridge. Stepping away I saw a dejected air over Rachel standing to the side. Sarah must have seen it too as we both went over to our ordinarily outspoken friend.

"Ladies, we can't say our last days in Weston weren't memorable." Sarah jokes trying to make light of just what occurred.

"Stop using the kid's gloves, I'm fine." Rachel mutters rolling her eyes. " And don't act like you both aren't happy I broke up with Cody. I know you hated him so jump in joy already. "

"What?" Sarah and I fake our surprises barely holding in our happiness. Yes, we are giddy that Rachel finally got rid of Cody. The man was scum and we could always see it and now she can too.

"Stop with the fake shock, your expression of joy is clear in your eyes." She mumbles, giving both of us hugs. "Thanks for not telling me I told you so about Cody."

"Always" we say hugging Rachel tighter. I can see the pain reflecting from her eyes as my friend tries to stay strong. This betrayal is a hard one for Rachel who only saw herself with Cody in the future. I wish I could activate my magic just to see what will come. However I found out of many other things waiting to be shown that are vital for all our futures

136

Laura the Healer

Trying to get my mind off of morbid things I decide to scan the village for other games I can play. Doing this for a couple of seconds something red catches my eyes. In the crowd stumbling is a young Native girl scarcely five feet tall wearing a red tribal dress.

"Laura." I was so excited to see my friend that I did not mind people gawking at me. Laura's gray eyes focus on me as she breathes a sigh of relief as I approach her.

"Andy, it's good to see you but let's get out of the crowd. These people's touches are getting really annoying." She complains as another person bumps into her earning a glare from her unseeing eyes..

Nodding my understanding at her irritation of being touched due to her blindness. Not having the ability to see Laura's sense of touch is very sensitive so she hates random people's touch. Putting my hand over her shoulder, I guided her over to the group. When we reach the others, Sarah practically tackles the smaller girl. "What are you doing here Laura, I thought you would miss the festival." She says squeezing Laura, whose head barely reached her chin.

"Father decided that we could leave early." Laura answers gazing at her friends with her sightless eyes.

"That's wonderful because we have much to tell you." Rachel replies, hugging Laura who looks like a child standing next to her.

"I know you do Rachel," Laura hints with a playful smirk that I recognized. She knows something that the rest of us didn't. I'm not the only one giving her a side look as Rachel joins me.

"Andy, who is your friend?" Jacob interrupts us, making us realize we forgot about the men when Laura appeared.

Blushing, I start the introductions. "I am sorry for our rudeness, but we were so happy to see her. This is our friend Laura Blackbird of the Shawkees tribe."

At hearing her name the men seemed to take a pause in shock and amazement, making me smile. "Laura Blackbird is the name of the diplomat that created the Bulkans treaty." Travis finally speaks up asking the question that is probably going through the others minds.

"Yes, I am the same Laura" Laura confirms her identity. With that discovery, the men gather around my friend in admiration.. Laughing I can't blame them Laura is a hero and an idol for what she had accomplished as a diplomat. She single handedly established the first treaty with the Bulkans, the most known non-diplomatic people around. The hero worship she's receiving is well deserved from the royals. Although oddly King Louis stands quietly to the side only observing Laura from afar.

"It's an honor to meet you in person," Mark greets Laura, shaking her hand. "Your work on the treaty was brilliant. My kingdom can trade without fear of the Bulkans stealing our supplies because of it."

Laura gives a tight smile and shrugs off the praise. "I am glad that the treaty is helping your people. However the original purpose was to aid the Natives allied to my father's tribe.". Nodding we knew the treaty was initially planned for an ally of Laura's father Nathaniel, who was having a problem with the Bulkans. The Bulkans, because of the war state, are always finding themselves in trouble. They raid nearby people for anything they can sell for income. The tribe allied with Laura's father were fur traders. Which was a high commodity in the north?

For a year, the tribe was helpless and finally asked Nathaniel for help. He was a negotiator to many different nomadic people and was highly sought after. However he was also the chief of his tribe so getting away to aid allies was difficult.

Stepping in, Laura negotiated a contract that allowed the Bulkans to get a small share of the trade with the promise of not attacking.

Both sides agreed, and the treaty worked so well other nations used it to settle matters with the Bulkans. The Watermark Compromise made Laura well known for being the first person to work successfully with the war nation.

"It might have been for your people, but it was able to help other nations" Mark replies looking into her eyes. He looks like he wants to bring them up but looks uncomfortable about the subject. Smiling, I know Laura is waiting for someone to reference the fact that she's blind. And luckily someone is brave enough to mention it.

"You're blind." Travis announces so bluntly that his brother smacks him on the side of his head.

"That's rude to say." Jacob says about to lecture his brother but is interrupted by chuckles.

The royals look stunned by Laura's laughter. "I was wondering when someone would mention my blindness," She explains. " Yes, I am blind, I have been since my birth. Let's get that out of the way. Don't feel strange around me because of it. I have adapted to it and my magic helps with sensing people around me." The royals look on as Laura walks up to each one of them showing how well she can move without sight.

"It is shocking that a person with your disability can accomplish so much." Travis blurts out not realizing what he said could be considered an insult.

At that comment I swear Jacob looks ready to punch his brother. "Travis, it's shameful to insult a woman of her honor." Jacob reprimanded his brother for his careless words but Laura didn't take any offense.

Waving off Jacob, Laura approaches Travis giving him her slyest smile. "You are a brash one, I think we can become good friends."

"See Jacob, she likes me" Travis brags still getting an evil eye from his brother.

"Yes, I do, your honesty is refreshing after dealing with stuffy leaders all day." Laura responds before adding. "And to answer your question, my blindness doesn't affect my hearing or my mind. I find a good mind and the ability to listen is a greater tool than sight can ever be in a negotiation." Her explanation is simple but has a quirkiness that makes each man satisfied with the answer. The celebrated diplomat has worked her magic again to diffuse a messy situation.

"Ms. Blackbird I'm King Louis of Petra." King Louis proclaims stepping up taking her hand. "And if it pleases you. I'd love to discuss treaties over dinner tonight." At that bold invitation the king makes it obvious he has an interest in my small friend. Though on the other hand Laura didn't pick up on the vibe only giving the king a shrug.

" Actually I plan to have dinner with my friends." Laura declines politely and without sight she misses how her rejection inflicted sorrow on the king's face. The King of Perta's whole demeanor seems shaken but he quickly recovers.

"Maybe you will have time later this week." He tries again, but a loud familiar voice overshadows everything else.

"Andy" Mel shouts out, appearing in front of us giving me a big hug. Stun my body freezes at her touch not knowing how to respond. Since moving out of my family's house two months ago Mel and I haven't spoken a word to each other.

"Mel, what are you doing?" I ask not even hiding my shock.

Mel only gives a giggle at my answer like I told a joke. "Just saying hello silly and by the way I love your dress it matches your eyes" she compliments.

I didn't know whether to say thank you or run away wondering if it was a trick. Removing myself from my sister's grasp in case she takes a swing at me. "Thanks Mel, and what a nice dress you have on also." I stammer out looking at what could be barely called a dress. The dress my sister wore is light blue with a tight bodice that pushed her breasts up for all to see. It also makes her waist look tinier and comes to Mel's knees showing off her smooth legs. My sister's attire didn't leave much to the imagination and I'm guessing that's what she's counting on.

Feeling relief when Mel turns her sights on King Louis completely forgetting about me. She sashays over to the King of Perta and starts batting her eyes.

"Wow, your sister lost her mind" Rachel whispers, coming to me watching Mel curtsy showing off her legs. Louis and Malcolm didn't seem to mind the view. However Mark and Jacob looked disturbed enough to walk away.

"How did she get out of the house without Father losing his mind?" I know if my father saw this he would have forbidden Mel to leave the house looking like that. " She must have snuck out before he saw her because there was no way my father would approve of that dress."

"I know. your sister looks like a." Rachel didn't even finish her sentence before Laura and Sarah began to look at something coming our way. A man stumbling is calling Laura by name with a large piece of glass in his right arm bleeding heavily.

"Laura, please help me." The man slurs but his eyes are becoming focused on my sister's chest. I recognize the man instantly as the shameless womanizer George Keller. He has a reputation of always flirting with young girls even with his wife standing next to him. I wouldn't be surprised if he got into a disagreement with one of the girls father's or husbands.

Laura walks up to the man and places her hands on his bleeding arm. Laura's magic specialty is healing, and with just one touch she can examine a wound. Closing her eyes, a blue light surrounds her hands and consumes George's arm.

Grimacing, I wince as blood gushes everywhere, some landing on Laura's dress. Yet my friend seems to be too focused on her patient to care. Everyone else is silently watching Laura work, but I can see Mel turning green at the sight.

Moving closer to Louis, Mel bats her eyes and smiles. "Laura can take care of this, why don't we get back to the festival. I can show you the sights" she offers leaning in to show off more of her breasts.

The King wasn't paying any notice of Mel's attempts at flirting. "I can't abandon Laura or my subject, but you can leave." He declares walking over with David behind him to look at the man's injury. I watch my sister pout and huff at the obvious rejection.

"I am a student healer for the Polla witches, maybe I can assist you." David volunteers looking at the man's arm in concern.

Laura only nods her concentration on the man's condition. "The glass is deep, but it didn't cause any internal injuries. Do you have any bandages to wrap his arm in?"

"Yes, I got that." David says, pulling out supplies from his traveling bag.

"Laura, is there something we can do?" asks Sarah.

"Hold him down, because I won't be able to numb him" she instructs. And with that we grab George's shoulders and push him to the ground.. Laura waits until we have him still before pulling out the glass slowly.

Keller screams and struggles breaking from our hold we had on him. "Let's help them restrain him" King Louis commands. And with that Malcolm and the king replaced us, easily securing the injured man's flailing limbs. Once the glass is out Laura uses her magic to stop the bleeding.

"David, bandage his injury please. My magic will stop the infection, but it still needs to be wrapped to heal properly" Laura orders. Listening, David begins bandaging the wound with George now looking relieved.

"What happened Mr. Keller? Did you get into a fight at the local pub again?" Rachel questions looking at the man as David ties the bandage in place.

"Honestly girls, I do not know" he groans. "I was walking around, and then that dust storm hit. I went for cover in this alley behind the pub. There I saw two large men talking, and then they started chasing me. I tripped and fell into a window. I must have blacked out because when I awoke I had this glass in my arm and the men were gone."

"That's weird, why would they chase you?" Sarah asks.

"I don't know, but they were foreigners by the accents. "

"Maybe you imagined it" Rachel proposes, rolling her eyes clearly not believing his story.

"'Maybe" George hisses as David makes quick work out of wrapping his arm. Getting up, George did look steadier but stumbled from his earlier drunkenness. Rotating his arms, "Thanks dear" he says swooping Laura up, giving her kisses all over her face.

"Rachel!" Laura yells as Rachel marches up to the drunken man.

She grabs his ear and twisted it making him shout in pain releasing Laura immediately. "Leave, before I tell your wife." She threatens as George turns white with fear before stumbling away.

"That man will never learn," Sarah groans, shaking her head.

"Hey, this time he didn't touch my bottom." Laura jokes amused but her joy is cut short as she begins to sway. Luckily King Louis who is directly behind Laura catches her before she can land. He quickly kneels, placing her on the ground with her head cradled in his lap. The moment seems almost romantic if my friend wasn't unconscious.

"Laura, wake up sweetie. "King Louis mumbles massaging her temples gently. At the term of endearment Rachel and I have twin expressions of disbelief. Did the King of Perta really just say that, did that mean he really likes Laura. Judging by the touching and his reaction right now I'm guessing my small friend ensnared his heart. Reaching for his canteen and splashing water on her face. Immediately, Laura's gray eyes fly open, alert but tired looking. Everyone gathers around taking a good look at her and Sarah is first to speak.

"Laura you over did it again." Sarah alleges pulling our friend up to sit. " You're in magical exhaustion." Upon hearing her diagnosis I can tell she's right. Laura was short of breath but her magical aura is weak that any witch around her knows the signs.. Magical exhaustion happens when a witch uses an enormous amount of their power at one time or for several days. One of the side effects of magical exhaustion is that the body doesn't have time to absorb any more magic. So in response it shuts down making the witch weary and sleepy for days.

"Yes, but I will be fine as soon as I eat." Laura tells us waving the concern away and getting back on her feet with some help from Sarah.

" Still you need to be aware of your limits. " Sarah scolds our small friend, earning an eye roll from Laura.

" Yes mother " Laura quips, earning a scowl from Sarah.

" Okay enough of this petty argument" King Louis says ending the disagreement. " Let's go get Laura some food." Not waiting on our answer King Louis takes Laura's hands and guides her to the direction of the food booths. Again we are left with our mouths open as the King of Perta makes a clear possessive claim on our small friend.

" Why do I get the feeling by the end of this day Laura might be engaged" Rachel whispers.

" I say by this afternoon he pops the question" Malcolm of Malloria guesses right beside her.

"That's kind, I wasn't even going to give them two hours. " I laugh with Malcolm and Rachel joining me. Turning around from the front of our group Laura stops walking, giving us a single glare.

" Remember my sight doesn't work so my strongest sense is my hearing. I would kindly ask people to stop taking bets on my personal life." She growls looking at us three in particular but her tone changes to sweet in the next sentence. " Now, which of my generous friends is going to lend me some money for food. "

" Did you just scold us and ask to borrow money at the same time?" Rachel mutters counting her money in her hand. " What happened this time? Did you forget your bag at home again."

" No " Laura grunts out. "I lost my bag, big difference."

"Who's turn is it to pay? I think I did it last time." Rachel says ignoring our friend's excuses, looking at Sarah and me.

Sarah only shakes her head and gives me a grin. "It's Andy's turn to pay. I did it before you Rachel.. "

Stomping my feet, I can imagine the significant dent it will have on my purse when another voice interrupts us. "I will pay for her food, so do not worry about it Andy." King Louis announces looking back at us smiling.

"You don't have to do that," Laura argues.

"Hey stay out of it, he is saving me coins." I yell out thanking the gods for what just happened. For a small person, Laura consumes a large amount of food and which in return costs me a lot of coins to feed her.

"Andy's right let him pay and next time it will still be her turn." Rachel counters earning a glare from me.

"Fine" Laura relents looking at the King. "Thank you, I appreciate it."

"No problem and this way we can get to know each other better." King Louis says with a smooth voice that would make a weaker girl swoon. Yet Laura just raises her eyebrow and shrugs it off.

"All right, but it better not be about treaties. I'm sick of hearing about them." She contends missing the king's flirting. Lifting her face, I can tell her nose is inhaling the smells around us. "The food smells good, let's go." She says going into the crowd bumping into everyone as she walks.

"Wait for us" Sarah shouts running after Laura. We follow after them and that's when I notice Mel is coming along with us. I wonder what her goal is since Mel cannot stand anyone in this group. Why would she be here voluntarily? That's the question on my mind. Looking determined I observe my sister trying to predict her end game, and then I see it. She maneuvers herself to be next to the King attempting to get his attention. I guess my sister hadn't given up yet on getting a royal. And if my guess is correct King Louis was her next target.

The Bulkans

The food booths of the Princess Festival are numerous in variety and quantity. It had something sweet for festival goers in the form of candy and donuts selling side by side. And if you desire something hearty they had ten different styles of chicken and beef courses to choose from. I'm just about to ask Laura what she wants to try first when I notice the sour expression on her face. Her face is tilted to the side and her nose starts to wrinkle like she inhaled something horrid.

At what she's smelling Laura's demeanor stiffen and she seems more alert.. I wasn't the only one noticing her actions. "Laura, what's the matter? "King Louis asks, touching her hand getting her attention.

"The Bulkans"she warns looking to the east as a man appears in the crowd. The man did have the Bulkans features with ice blue eyes and a gigantic body for which the nation is known for. His size is a little frightening that the nearby people begin to distance themselves from him. He didn't seem to mind gliding proudly to our direction with a certain confidence in his air.

"Laura, I've been looking for you everywhere." The stranger announces grinning at Laura like he caught his prey.

"Alek, I did not know you were coming here." She greets the man with a strain smile.

"I heard about the festival from a couple of my men and decided to check it out. It was sort of a last minute choice but seeing you here it must be fate." Alek suavely answers before looking around realizing there are other people present.. "Where are my manners? I am Alek Cuka of Bulka and who are you may I ask?"

"I am Andy Miller, and this is Sarah Palmer and Rachel Goodman. We're friends of Laura" I respond, eyeing the man up close. Alek to my knowledge seems to be in his late thirties or early forties with graying long blond hair that lands on his muscular shoulders. He has scars on his cheeks, neck, and stomach that I can see through the leather buttoned vest he wore. The swords and knives strapped to him seem to compliment his attire. Alek's height matches Malcolm's, but he didn't have the kindness in his blue eyes that the young general possesses.

"Of course, the seer and the elemental witches. My Laura talks about you girls often." Alek remarks, shaking our hands and I'm silently glad when he lets go soon after. Something about this man makes me dislike him, especially the way he speaks about Laura. It's like she is a possession, not a person. Just thinking about this makes me remember something Laura once confided with me about. It was a couple of days after she returned from negotiating the Bulkans treaty. She was visibly shaken about an encounter with a Bulkan's general. Apparently the man became so enamored with her he began following her everywhere. She couldn't be out of his sight or the man would start fights like a jealous lover. It was so bad Laura had to sneak back to Perta in the cover of night just to escape the fellow..

I hoped the incident was behind her but by looking at Laura's face the nightmare came back.

"I am King Louis of Perta, welcome to my land." King Louis announces pulling my focus off my friend and to their conversation. Upon hearing the king's title Alek looks at Louis sizing him up before offering his hand to shake.

"Nice to meet you, your Majesty," Alek declares but the way he says it makes the hairs of my arm stand up. The others did their introductions to Alek, but you can tell the tension is tight in our group.

"It's nice to meet so many royals and their ladies but none as beautiful as my Laura." Alek alleges touching Laura's face making her recoil slightly.

"Oh, how sweet," Mel says snidely, giving Laura a smirk. "Why don't you lovebirds get out of here and spend time together." My sister suggests leaning closer to King Louis as she says that. Scowling I can tell my sister is scheming to get rid of Laura to ensure the King's attention will be squarely on her.

At that idea Laura is about to object until Louis intervenes, taking her hand and squeezing it. "It's been great meeting you but we should get going. Laura is exhausted and requires rest so you enjoy the festival." Even though it's polite it is still a clear dismissal.

"If my Laura needs something, I will get it." Alek argues looking hostile at King Louis who is holding Laura's hand.

"No, I think I'm more than qualified to handle Laura's needs." Louis counters knowing what he just implied. Alek stomps forward about to meet the King if Laura didn't throw her small body in between the men.

"Alek, I can speak with you some other time." She offers to try to appease the man.

"My dear, I can't accept your answer. I want you to be with me and only me.." Alek demands grabbing Laura's arm and pulling her to his side. At these actions Louis reacts quickly elbowing the man in his chest severing his grip. Laura is released and placed behind King Louis' back so Alek cannot grab her again.

Drawing out his sword, Alek starts to advance on Louis. "Give her to me boy, before things get ugly for you." Snorting, the King of Perta just glances at the sword in front of him like it's a toy.

"Don't be stupid, do you want to start a war Bulka cannot handle?" Louis' voice is so calm you can barely tell his life is endangered. Alek looks at Louis dumbstruck, but his rage comes back getting ready to strike.

"What is going on here?" A familiar voice yells as I turn around to see my father coming towards us with Ella beside him.

"Father, it's good to see you." I declare going over to hug him. Once I'm close enough I whisper in his ear. "This is getting out of hand, please diffuse it quickly." Letting go after delivering the message I pretend that all is well. I watch Father nod his understanding heading over to the conflict in question.

"Hello gentlemen, what seems to be the problem here?" Father inquires his eyes examining the sword in Alek's hand. Both men must have realized my father's importance because Alek lowers his blade.

"This man is trying to take what is mine." He accuses Louis.

"Laura isn't yours and the festival states any royal can claim her." Louis challenges and with that Alek in fury lunges at the king. Luckily Malcolm, who was silent until now intervenes grabbing the large man pulling him away from King Louis..

"That's enough, I order you all to stop this madness. The Princess Festival is meant to be a peaceful event not one of bloodshed. If you cannot act civilly I will be forced to ban you all from the village do you understand. " Father commands, making his stance clear as the tension melts and both men look resigned to agree.

"Fine. I'll let the matter drop for now, but it isn't over" Alek promises.

"Noted," Louis agrees, his eyes cold.

"Well this is an exciting day to be out," Ella jokes with a nervous smile. Looking at my mother for the first time in two months she seems like her usual self but dressed better. Today she wore a long flowing aqua color dress that is stitched to make her waist small and bust bigger.. Her long blond hair is curled up and if I didn't know better. I say my mother was the one looking for a husband.

"Melissa, what are you wearing?" Father fumes his face dismayed looking at Mel's attire. I guess I was right Mel must have left the house before father was able to see her.

"I know, Andrew, she looks fabulous." Ella interjects before my father can get angrier. "What do you say, sir, does my daughter not look beautiful?" Ella asks Alek who is looking at my sister's breast that had almost fallen out.

"Yes, she is like a pretty flower," he compliments, giving Mel's hand a kiss."

Fanning her face, Mel gives him a blush and begins fawning over Alek. Touching his muscles and stroking his ego Ella watches on pleased. "Your mother and sister are quite a pair." Jacob comments looking at both blonds throwing themselves at Alek. Shaking my head in shame, not even minutes ago Mel was all over Louis.

"Maybe we'll get lucky, and both will leave together." Rachel proposes looking at the two with disgust.

"I don't think so Rachel." Malcolm replies standing beside her. "They're' not going to leave until they get what they think belongs to them." His words ring true that I didn't need my foresight to predict their accuracy.

"I hope you aren't disappointed that Melissa changed her mind about you." Rachel voices out looking at Malcolm with a smirk.

"Not at all, she's a little small for me. I need a woman of solid stock. " Malcom states looking directly at my friend's tall and womanly body.

Glaring, she brushes off his obvious flirting to press on with the questioning. "I couldn't tell by the way you were gawking at her chest earlier."

Shrugging Malcolm remarks unapologetic. "Her breasts were on display, what man would not look if they had a chance?"

"Pig." Rachel accuses and Malcolm acts hurt by her remark and the two are back to arguing.

"They should just kiss." Jacob proposes smiling at one of the comments the two are throwing at each other.

"Don't you think that might be too soon, her heart just got crushed by Cody." I warn my fiance not wanting my friend to get hurt for the second time.

"I think that heartbreak was for the best in the long run. Honestly I believe Rachel's heart will heal soon and a famed general might be her new love." Jacob hints the last part towards Malcolm.

"We don't know if Malcolm is even interested in her." I respond but only get laughter at my response from my fiancé.

" Andy, you must be blind" Jacobs says, still chuckling. "The only reason Malcolm is still with us is Rachel. He hasn't moved more than two feet away from her since the time they met.

"Really" I verbalize thinking back and realizing Jacob is correct. Since meeting Malcolm has never really left Rachel's side. The giant is always a couple of steps behind or directly across from her. And not to mention the obvious flirting he is throwing at my friend at their little quarrel now is quite telling.

"What's going on over here?" Laura asks as she joins us with Louis not far behind.

"Andy finally realized Malcolm is smitten with Rachel" Jacob blurts out.

"And they say I'm blind." She teases me before turning her head to where Rachel and Malcolm are standing. "The emotions coming from them are strong. I believe with time and patience they will be a perfect match."

Hearing that it makes me feel a lot better about the future. Thankfully Laura does not only have a healing ability but she's an empath. She can perceive others emotions that are near her and it comes in handy at times like this.

"So, you can sense emotions too?" King Louis says and when Laura nods he continues. "Can you sense my feelings right now towards you.." He questions boldly making Jacob and I gasp.

At that remark Laura becomes red in embarrassment probably just realizing the king's affections. It's entertaining to watch my friend navigate this sticky situation I thought in my head. "This is very flattering and I think it's sweet you are interested in me. However I can't be with a man who isn't confident" she professes.

King Louis frowns at Laura's scathing comments and I feel suddenly awkward listening now. "We should leave." I whisper to Jacob wanting to give the two some privacy but my fiancé remains in the same spot.

"Why? This isn't exactly a private place and I want to hear what Laura tells him." Jacob responds and continues to listen to the conversation between the two.

"What are you talking about? I'm the King of Perta, of course I'm confident." King Louis argues but Laura just shakes her head smiling sadly at him.

"Being confident doesn't mean being arrogant." She says honestly, giving the king a hard stare. "Louis, since your mother has been gone you haven't created one new law. Also it took you three years to visit the west, one of your mother's most treasured accomplishments. Weston wouldn't be in dire straits if you took charge sooner." She didn't sugarcoat her opinions on Louis' decisions in the kingdom, making what she says impactful.

Her words must have touched a nerve because King Louis is speechless now. "Okay, she just loaded into him. " Malcolm remarks after hearing the end of Laura's speech.

"Yeah, I got to admit Laura was harsher than usual" Rachel comments looking at the King with sympathy. "Poor guy, I wouldn't be surprised if he just leaves right now."

"He'll stay. I think this is exactly what he wanted." Malcolm replies confidently watching Louis just stare at Laura with a severe expression. Only when he is about to speak Ella and Father comes rushing up to us with Mel hanging off Alek's arm.

"Melissa told us about George and about Laura needing to replenish her strength." Father declares walking up to Laura giving the girl a look of concern." How are you sweetie?"

"Fine Mr. Miller, you know how the healing goes." Laura says dismissively even though she looks still tired.

Seeing that Father frowns and let my friend lean against him. "Let's go get something to eat. It's been a long day. I think food is what we all need. "

" Great idea father." Mel cheers hanging off Alek's arm at the same time giving Louis a ton of flirty stares . After that everyone moves in the direction of the food with Father in the lead. I follow along with the others feeling like something is going to happen today that will change everything I once knew.

Ella's Ambition

Sitting at the center square of Weston our group gathered after getting Laura some food. The area is filled with happy people enjoying the festival with the exception of my father. "That dirty scumbag." He growls as I just finish telling him what happened to Tim.

"Scumbags since his sons are traitors also." Rachel points out right next to us reminding us of Cody's and Matthew's involvement.

"I still cannot believe that the Walkers did this "Father says, perplexed. "They had everything in Weston, why throw it away."

"Whatever their reasons are, I'm happy I don't have to marry Matthew now." Mel celebrates in happiness, missing the disturbed expressions she's receiving. To think of an engagement being canceled is heartless when talking about treason from a trusted ally. Clueless of the animosity she is getting, Mel continues her celebration by flirting with Alek. "Now that I am a free woman again, who'll be my next lover." She hints and Alek didn't seem bothered by my sister's conduct.

Instead, he's taking advantage of her willingness to please him. "I am sure I can arrange something but I'm a little perched. Can you get me some lemonade" he asks?

"Of Course," Mel volunteers sashaying away making sure Alek is watching. The lemonade stand is a couple yards away and it has a long line. Alek gazes at Mel with mild amusement that she ate up. Shaking my head at the pair I can't help but be confused by this development.

Deciding to take a break from their drama I turn to see my mother glaring at Laura. Scowling I can't see a reason why until I notice my friend is sitting directly next to King Louis. Knowing Ella she probably plans on Mel being the one to entice the king not Laura.

"King Louis, I'm sorry about what happened between Tim and his family. My mother declares moving forward to be by the king's side forcing Laura out of her seat. Once that occurs I see my mother grin at seeing Laura's retreating form.

"Rude" Laura mutters moving to another seat.

"The Walker matter needed to be addressed, and I'm glad I was able to help Weston." Louis answers, giving Laura a pointed look before he adds. "Even though some people here have strong opinions of me ignoring the village for so long." At that remark Laura only rolls her eyes making the king grin.

"Hogwash. Ella protests missing Louis grinning at Laura. "That's ridiculous I bet you had too much work to do in the capital."

At that comment King Louis looks generally thoughtful." Yes I have been busy since taking the throne and that's why I am here at the Princess Festival. I want to find a wife that can shoulder the burden with me and be my partner." He confesses in a sincere voice that makes me realize how many struggles this young king has to carry. Maybe that's why he is so interested in Laura; she's an ideal choice. Not only does she have knowledge on policies and treaties, something that the king can use in the future. Her reputation would also be an added bonus by his side.

Everyone else must be thinking similar thoughts but one person. " My daughter Melissa would be the perfect choice for you." Ella proposes shocking us all by her words. " She's good with people and is very kind." She lies, earning a snort from me and giggles from Rachel.

That fib wasn't even believable to the king. Who previously witnessed my sister's uncaring nature when talking about her engagement. "Oh, really? Can she negotiate treaties and counsel our people in crisis" Louis questions pointedly?

"Of course not, Melissa knows her place is in the household not doing men's work." Ella disputes looking offended that the king proposed such a thing.

"That's the wife I require and if we are speaking on this matter alone. Laura is a better choice than your daughter" Louis declares.

"It's not right! A woman's place is at home tending to her family." Ella argues with the king. " No respectful girl would travel around getting into men's business. " She preaches throwing an obvious insult at Laura who only laughed it off.

"Oh, Mrs. Miller, are you talking about me?"

"Yes, a woman should be home with children not getting into all types of trouble." Ella rants turning her stare back on the king. "King Louis my daughter is the exact woman all of Perta should strive to be. Not someone who is running around trying to get people to sign a paper." At that remark the humor left Laura's face as she marched up to my mother giving her a cold glare.

"That paper saved hundreds if not thousands of people." Laura disagrees with her voice getting louder with each word. "If your definition of a woman means I can't save lives then so be it. I'll be a freak but I will never give up my work as a diplomat." Clapping is heard next as Louis interrupts the two women's confrontation. The King of Perta has a soft expression on his face as he moves to separate Laura from my mother.

"Well said Laura." He proclaims before taking her hand, turning to Ella and saying. " I made my decision of what kind of wife I desire. And the person who fits that category is Laura who will soon be my queen." The announcement alarms everyone including Laura and Ella both snapping their heads back .

"What?" Alek begins standing up but luckily Malcolm is there grabbing the man's shoulder.

"Don't even think about it or you'll be facing the General of Falcon Ridge." The threat must have stupefied Alek because he freezes in place.

"That was you?" He asks, looking at Malcolm like he saw a ghost.

"Yes, and I'd rather not let this nice festival turn into a battlefield." Malcolm responds, his eyes cold as he gestures to the guards surrounding them. Grunting, Alek turns to leave but not before he bumps shoulders with Malcolm.

"Looks like you made a new friend," Rachel teases.

"I just cannot hide my dislike for that man" Malcolm announces. While this is going on I almost missed Ella's reaction to Louis's news.

"She's blind why choose her over my daughter? "Ella spat out and I can see her hopes are dwindling as she adds. "Your Highness, if you marry Laura then your future heirs could be as blind as she is."

"My children are none of your concern and for your information. I have the best healers in the kingdom that can cure a child of blindness in the womb." Louis declares taking, insult of my mother's comment about Laura. .

"You wouldn't have to risk that if you marry my daughter. " Ella tries to persuade the king . "She can give you plenty of healthy babies to be heirs." That part she practically screams out like that will help her case. It only worsened her situation in my opinion as King Louis openly scowls at my mother in hatred.

"Ella, this is enough. Melissa will get married but not to a royal." Father interjects stepping in as Ella becomes more unhinged at Louis' continuous refusal.

"My baby deserves better than marrying a farmer." She screams in fury as her eyes turn to one person .. "This is all her fault." Pointing an accusing finger at Laura like she has done a great wrong. Suddenly the wind picks up and a familiar aura appears over Ella's body. I shiver with the temperature dropping instantly as my mother's magic increases. Dark skies materialize and the sound of cracking thunder can be heard . "I am not going to let her win." Ella raises her hand in the air making chairs fly because of the wind. Screaming people ran out of the way trying to dodge rubble and other items.

"Ella stop, you are going to hurt someone." Louis orders as he tries to restrain her. Seeing him come towards her my mother sends a strong gust of wind at Louis. It pushes him back into a couple booths twenty feet away. After that She creates a funnel of air to spin around her. It prevents anyone else from coming near her to stop this madness.

"I'll just get rid of her then King Louis will have no choice but to marry Melissa." She announces shocking me as I realize her true motive. The funnel of air shifts around her picking up chairs and tables around us. These objects are all being propelled towards my small defenseless friend.

"Laura" I scream watching the chairs and table being hurled at her not being able to help. Just when they are going to make contact, rocks and stones from nearby buildings fly around Laura. Together the rocks create a dome-shaped shelter shielding her from the attack.

Turning to the source of the magic I see Rachel preserving the dome. Ella, furious at her plan being stopped, turns her efforts on Rachel. With her attention on Rachel, she overlooks the water from a nearby fountain flowing like a snake with Sarah controlling it. Molding the water with her magic into a ball, Sarah throws it at a distracted Ella.

It hit my mother square in the stomach knocking her to the ground. Hurt, and losing control of her magic the storm finally vanishes. Waiting a minute Rachel scans the sky for signs of Ella's magic. Seeing that the magic is gone, she releases the barrier over Laura. Rocks and stones that once was a dome come crashing to the ground missing the trembling girl they were protecting seconds ago.

Stumbling out in a confusion, Laura almost trips over the rocks. "Laura, are you all right?" I yell running to her checking for any injuries. Luckily there was nothing. Rachel's quick actions saved our friend's life.

"I'm fine, thank heavens for Rachel." Laura weeps in relief.

Rubbing her head "It's all right." I sooth calmly even though it was a big lie. My mother had done something unforgivable to a kind and giving girl. For what so a royal would notice my sister is unbelievable.

"She is getting up." Someone shouts pointing to Ella as she gets to her feet. Finally standing she is surrounded by guards with their blades at her neck. Sinking back to her knees, my mother seems to finally understand what her actions have cost her.

"Please don't hurt me" she begs holding up her hands.

"Laura, are you hurt?" Louis asks, checking her for any wounds. Once it's established that Laura is not damaged. He holds her hand tightly looking at my mother groveling on the ground for mercy. Although by the king's demeanor the last thing he wants to give is mercy. "Mercy has long passed for you." Louis pointing his own sword at my mother's throat. "Your crimes don't deserve any leniency for attempting to kill an innocent woman." Falling apart, Ella tries to grab one of Louis's pants legs but is swiftly detained. Chains are secured around her wrist and ankles so every movement is controlled. Feeling that my mother's time is up I can't help but get a question off my mind.

"Mother, why did you even try to harm Laura?" My voice is steady, not letting my emotions of anger out. A hand on my shoulder keeps as Jacob's tight grip seems to be the only thing keeping me from attacking Ella myself.

My voice must have done the trick because even in chains Ella morphs back to her usual self. "I was trying to obtain a King for your sister after the one you stole from us" Ella alleges her eyes cold.. "For a waste of space to be picked over my baby is unacceptable. And I wasn't going to let your friend ruin another chance for my dreams to come true." My mind is in shock, and I wasn't the only one at Ella's confession. I didn't know what to say after this, but someone did.

"Ella, how could you do this?" Father speaking in disapproval at his wife's actions alongside many others. It's well-known Ella could be nasty but attempting to kill someone out of jealousy is unbelievable.

"Andrew, she was taking a King away from our daughter." Ella argues, not comprehending that killing Laura was a crime. I wonder how far gone was my mother's logic to believe this was alright..

"I've heard enough" Louis snaps his voice, stopping every other person around them. "You wanted a King for your daughter, now one will be locking you away to stand trial." His words make Ella's bravado dissolve as she falls apart when guards begin taking her away.

Panicking, Ella's eyes had that familiar glow to them. However a sword placed at her heart quickly silences any resistance. I stare at Ella being forced to stand before I look at my Father who is shell-shocked. He didn't seem capable of processing anything, and when Mel comes running up, I think it finally clicked in his mind.

"Melissa" Father shouts in horror when my sister confronts the guards holding Ella.

"Let go of her" Mel yells, swinging her fist at one of the guards. At her actions some of the men even start to point their weapons at her and Louis intervenes thankfully.

"Melissa, stop this right now or face imprisonment with your mother." That statement halts all further attempts for my sister.

"What did she do?" Mel questions looking at everyone for an answer as people remained silent. No one wants to respond to the question except Louis.

"She tried to kill Laura." Louis replies and with a clap of his hands the guards restart taking my mother away.

Mel watches this horrified before looking at my father for help. "Daddy, do something. Don't let them take her away." At my sister's tears I realize her whole life is falling apart like our mother's. To Mel Ella isn't just her mother but her best friend so this must be terrible to her.

Father who must have had similar thoughts because his shoulder straightens up. Determined he walks up to King Louis and stands before him. "King Louis, please wait a moment. "

"This better not be about lessening your wife's crimes because I will not turn a blind eye." Louis states his eyes unsympathetic. I see Father's shoulders becoming tense at this moment.

"I understand her crimes need to be answered for," Father announces, shocking Mel. "I am only asking for my wife to be detained at my house instead of jail for my daughters' benefit." Nodding, Mel agrees, but I didn't say a word. The last thing I wanted is to be in the same room as an attempted murderer.

"I am not going to be merciful." King Louis refuses but is interrupted by Laura.

Looking small but undaunted, she speaks. "Let Ella go home instead of jail. She'll still be put on trial and be sentenced to banishment or worse." Her surprise defense of my mother stuns all of us including King Louis.

"Laura, she tried to kill you," he says.

"And Rachel saved me, and now I want to show kindness." Laura announces marching up to Ella giving her an unfriendly stare. "This isn't for you but your family Ella. I wouldn't care if you were struck dead right now. However Andrew wants this and I will give him this request." And with that speech she looks at Louis waiting for his answer.

"Laura, are you sure?" Louis states and when Laura nods he relents. "I guess you got lucky Ella, you can go home for now." Mel and Ella cried in relief thinking she escaped punishment but it's short lived. "Nevertheless after the festival, you will be transferred to the capital and imprisoned with the Walkers.. At that my sister and mother's faces are shattered again as their hopes disappear. To be placed with the Walkers my mother will be labeled just as horrible as they are.

"I don't think that's fair" Mel protests, but father interjects.

"That is more than fair, my King." Father declares silencing my sister and taking charge of the arrangement of placing Ella at home. Mel seems furious at father's acceptance but hides her displeasure thankfully. Instead she glares at Laura like she's the cause of all this. Disgusted with my family playing the victim while the real one was standing by herself terrified. Turning to look at Laura, I see Alek there leaning over her whispering something in her ear. Whatever it is it upsets Laura to the point she turns chalky and pale.

Frowning, I move to go to her side, but Jacob grabs my hand. "Andy, your father is asking if you wanted to say goodbye to your mother."

Looking at my mother, I can honestly say I would rather eat dirt than do that. ""No, I'm done with her." I answer, writing off Ella from my life. Jacob agrees and signals the guards to usher my family away. The villagers spread out making a path so wide that twenty men can walk side by side.

Ella, now in chains and shackles walks awkwardly with her head down. Her festival dress is dirty, and her hair lost its curl. She's a completely different person than the woman who's the village leader's wife. Ella Miller was once respected and awed, now she is notorious. As if she knows her reputation is gone. She lifts her eyes to meet mine and a look of revenge greets me. By that one look I acknowledged that my mother truly hated me and wanted payback. And by this day's end Ella got her wish at the cost of others.

Accusations

Once my mother is escorted away and the crowd finally disperses. All I can think of is Ella and what her crime meant for my whole family. My family's name will be tarnished and worse my father might lose his position as the leader of Weston. All these things keep running through my head making me miss Sarah running up to me.

"Andy" she hollers

"Sarah what is it?"

"Something is wrong with Laura. Alek threatened her" Sarah replies pulling me over to Laura who looks shaken.

"Laura, tell us what happened." Rachel insists on rubbing Laura's shoulder as the smaller girl looks ready to fall apart.

Tears in her eyes she chokes out. "He says to enjoy the boy King's affection because soon you will be mine." Feeling a shiver go over me. Something about these words were ominous and troubling. It's as if my body is foreshadowing something terrible is going to occur.

"I am going to kill him." Rachel shrieks balling up her fist looking ready to fight. I scan the crowd for signs of Alek just in case Rachel flies off the handle.

"He's gone, he left when the men were occupied," Laura informs us, guessing my thoughts. At that the tension I feel wash away. Something about that man makes me apprehensive. It's like there's more to his motivation to be here than Laura.

"Laura, we should tell King Louis. He will order Alek out of Weston" Sarah replies. I nod at the plan already in motion to go to the king, but Laura blocks me.

"Stop," she says, rubbing her eyes. "I just want to forget about it." Looking at each of us she gives a pleading stare. "It might be nothing and we're probably overreacting. Louis is already dealing with a lot without us adding our paranoia." I shake my head in disagreement thinking we should tell him anyway but Laura might have a point. Alek is probably bluffing trying to scare Laura. And the King does have more pressing problems including my mother and the Walkers to deal with.

"Fine but if he tries anything. I'm going to bury him" Rachel warns looking at the men returning to us. Releasing a breath, Laura mouths the words thank you.

"I cannot believe you showed that woman mercy." King Louis exclaims when he comes over to Laura.

"She is only staying at her home until the festival is over, not getting a pardon." Laura argues before glaring at Louis. "And what did you mean about making me your wife?" Louis to his credit didn't shrink away meeting her stare.

"I know nothing's wrong with your hearing so exactly what I said" he asserts.

" I don't even like you, why pick me." Laura complains ignoring all the shock gasps of the crowd for defying the King of Perta.

"Shame" the King of Perta challenges with a laugh. "You have until the festival's last day to get to know your future husband." Laura, true to her nature, stays calm at his remark.

Putting on a forced smile Laura relents, accepting her fate. "Well I cannot deny a claim because of the festival rules." And with that Louis pulls out a ruby ring with the royal crest engraved in it. Putting it on Laura did something that surprised everyone present. "Hey, Rachel, is this ring ugly?" She yells out lifting her finger to show off the ring.

Laughter fills the group as Louis rolls his eyes like it doesn't faze him. "It is very pretty, I have good taste."

"I'm blind and no offense. I'd rather have my friend's opinion." Laura responds looking at Rachel for her answer. "Rachel, tell me the truth is this thing hideous. I cannot wear something ugly for the rest of my life." She rants in a serious voice making Louis scowl at her comments.

Chuckling, Rachel comes forward inspecting the ring meticulously and even whistling at the end.

"It's pretty, but you can always ask for better." My tall friend answers with a fake snotty voice making us chuckle.

"Hey, at least you get a ring.." I grumble out waving my empty hand in the air.

Feeling a pinch on my side making me jump. Jacob appears next to me giving a stern face. "If you must know Andy. The ring is stunning and has been in the royal family for generations."

"So, it's old," Rachel comments, earning a friendly shove from Jacob.

"That's enough ladies, we are stealing the moment away from Louis. Now Laura please, give this poor man an answer before he bursts over here." Jacob states gesturing to Louis as the man looks crossed from waiting.

"Jacob's right, do not leave that poor man hanging." Rachel urges Laura back over to the king to accept the proposal. Once the yes was said, the audience thrilled and shouted for a kiss. Louis happily gives them their wish, taking my small friend in his arms. The kiss is sweet at first but after a couple seconds it looks like a make out session.

"Okay, he is taking this a little too far." Rachel mumbles as Louis seems to be enjoying the kiss very much. Although from my viewpoint, Laura didn't seem to mind his affection.

However a well-placed kick to the shins proved me wrong. "No touching until you talk to my Father." Laura mandates turning her back to Louis but her face is flush. "Girls,where are we going next?" At that announcement Laura is back to her giddy self.

"Hay maze!" Jordan yells, grabbing at Rachel's sleeve impatiently. "You promised to take me this year sissy." He reminds her with a frown on his face.

"What is the hay maze?" David inquires adjusting his glasses"

"The hay maze is a bunch of stacks of hay made into a labyrinth that idiots go into every year." Sarah answers in a grumpy mood. In my opinion the hay maze is fun but Sarah's opinion is a little biased. It comes from an incident when we were younger when she got lost in it.

"Sarah, it was seven years ago let it go," Rachel grunts out.

"Let it go " Sarah shouts, giving Rachel the evil eye. " I was stuck in that nightmare for five hours by myself."

"That was a pure accident" Laura says with a small chuckle.

"Who's fault was that accident" she accuses glaring at all of us girls.

"It was ours, but we thought you were right behind us" Rachel argues in defense of our actions.

"You three walked off when I took a break" Sarah alleges. "And I only got out because Grandma Ruth found me with her sight." I can't help but giggle at the memory of our ten year old selves walking the hay maze for the first time. We were so excited that the three of us accidentally left poor Sarah behind. After that we went to Grandma Ruth to save the day and we got a scolding for leaving a friend behind.

"Come on Sarah, it will be fun. And this time we will not leave you." Rachel promises, hugging our mad friend.

"Fine," Sarah agrees, rolling her eyes. We're about to walk off together when the loud clearing of throats halt our progress. There, standing every bit annoyed are the scowling men that we had forgotten about again.

"We'd like to go to this maze too," Mark announces for the men. Making us blush the men begin following us to the outskirts of Weston where the maze is located. As we travel the stands and booths become less and less. We're nearing the brewery when I notice a few villagers throwing me side glances. Some would even point and say unflattering things about me as I passed them. Feeling like a pariah, I speed up my pace hoping I can outrun the gossipers.

Just when the gate comes into view two familiar wisps of girls block my way. Seeing their long brown hair, long faces and a beauty mark on their cheek. I groan at seeing Molly and Rebecca Sanders, the twins of Weston and pains in my side. The sisters never really liked me for some reason and accused me of thinking I was better than them. Even though I tried numerous times to make friends with them.

I move to pass the sisters but Molly steps into my path. "Oh Andy you aren't leaving?" She prods in that snarky voice of hers.

"Of course she is my sister. Andy is probably running home to cry about her mother being arrested." Rebecca taunts me while I just bite my tongue staying quiet. There's nothing I can say to these girls to change their opinions. They have already made up their minds about me and my family. It's a waste of effort to get drawn into a senseless fight with them so I remain silent.

"The great Andy Miller has nothing to say" Molly snorts, lifting her nose at me. "The girl who walked around with her mouth flying open is silent who would have guessed."

"Leave her alone" Rachel snaps coming over to us. Her size and demeanor alone seems to make the sisters falter a little, but not entirely.

"Why? Her family has been all-mighty for years and now they are in disgrace" Rebecca alleges. The villagers around us seemed to get louder at every remark the girl made my way. I'm saddened at the responses the villagers are giving me. After all the things my father and grandmother did over the years for the people of Weston. The actions of Ella tarnished our whole family in one day erasing all the good deeds that the Millers have done for generations. I'm about to yell at Rebecca and her friends but stop. I know it will cause my father more trouble in the future . Slipping past the sisters I try to ignore them but they continue to follow me like vultures.

"And let's not forget her fiancés family, the traitor" Rebecca laughs.

"I haven't even met my fiancés family yet except his younger brother." I reply letting that little remark come out without meaning it. Biting my tongue, I walk faster trying not to say anything else.

"Liar, you knew Matthew your whole life" Molly accuses. And with that people in the crowd mumbles their agreement.

"No dear, you are mistaken because I'm Andy's fiancé." Jacob proclaims stepping up to the teasing girls and bowing. "Let me introduce myself. "I' m King Jacob of Polla" Jacob letting his title run through the crowd. The twins and their followers kneel immediately.

"It's an honor to meet you." Rebecca stammers quickly looking down while her sister remains quiet with their posse.

"I cannot say the same." He responds, glaring at the twins making them gulp. "Now I'll be very grateful if you both stop harassing my future queen." Jacob says coldly, grabbing my hand and leading me away from the now wide-eyed girls.

"You didn't have to interfere, I had it under control." I claim but snorting from Rachel and Laura saying they disagree with me.

"I know but the look on her face when I said my title was priceless," Jacob laughs.

"That was funny and thank you." I reply, kissing him on the cheek before I'm forced away. Glaring at Rachel who is the cause of it.

"Don't give me that look you can smooch later." She says, giving me a playful shove forward.

"Rachel, I think Andy is starting to ignore us since she got a boyfriend," Laura alleges in a teasing voice.

" How sweet, our little red-haired demon is finally getting some love." Rachel announces loudly, getting chuckles at my expense. "

"That's it, I am getting new friends!"

"You can't get rid of us." Sarah comments giving me a one-armed hug. "Andy, you're stuck with us for life." Taking comfort in that, I take on my friends' cheerful mood as we approach the hay maze. The maze is magnificent, taking up a hundred acres. Originally the maze was designed as a scavenger hunt based on a story of a labyrinth and red string. Yet over time it became the center point of the festival. So every year the elders in charge of the maze reinvent clues to excite a new generation.

"Let's go" Jordan hollers in excitement.

"Before we go in, maybe we should go in pairs. This way no one will get lost" Laura explains.

"That's a good idea." Rachel states already putting the idea in place. "Okay, Sarah, you and Mark can go with Andy and Jacob. The boys can go together and that leaves four people that can be the last group."

"Sissy, I want to go with Andy." Jordan demands as only a seven-year-old boy can.

"Fine, go with Andy" she says as Jordan runs up and hugs me. "Any questions or does this plan work for everyone."

"Sounds good to me" Sarah replies.

"Okay, let's go." Rachel directs, leading us to the maze entrance. The maze is almost deserted this year except for us and a few people.

"Rachel, your group should go in first." Jacob says, looking at the maze with excitement. For once, my King looks happy about something that wasn't attached to my face.

"All right, see you when I'm out of the maze girls," Rachel waves her goodbyes leading Malcolm, Laura, and Louis into the maze. After five minutes the boys went next followed by my group shortly after. Feeling confident, I'm confident I'll get out first and rub it in Rachel's and Laura's faces. If only I could predict in four hours how my life was going to change.

The Vision

The sun is bearing down on the five of us in the hay maze of horror which is what I'm calling it in my head. Four hours have passed with us not getting any closer to finding a way out. My small group looks tired leaning on the stacks of hay in defeat.

"Andy, I hate you right now." Sarah moans sitting on the ground. Mark is right next to her trying to be uplifting, but failing when Sarah gives him a stink eye.

"Sarah, don't be angry, we'll get out of here. " I reply, searching for any sign of an exit.

"Andy admit it, we've been going in circles." Sarah yells hysterically, waving her arms at the endless turns that we had already been through.

" Fine we're lost" I concede, kicking at the ground in frustration. The only one who still seems animated is Jordan as he babbles on to Jacob who is entertaining the child. To be young and unaware of being lost is a gift I thought.

"I wish I didn't come in this maze again," Sarah whines, laying her head on the hay. I'm about to say we should head back to the entrance when a loud explosion almost shatters my eardrum. The ground vibrates and more loud booms echo around us. Looking up and seeing smoke that appears to be coming from the village.

"What is going on!" Mark shouts looking at the smoke.

"I don't know, but we should get out of here." Jacob says as my eyes start to blur as the path out of the maze is shown to me. Somehow, the chaos initiated my magic and I can see the path to freedom.

The exit I estimate is ten yards from us. "Follow me, my sight has shown me the way out." I yell running off before anyone can argue.

Hearing thundering footsteps behind me, I'm happy the others are following behind.

In a surreal state, I feel my magic pulling me along like an invisible thread and I can't stop. When the exit comes into view the power decreases but is still there as my normal eyesight returns. Once we go through the exit, everyone is out of breath but no one says a word. We're speechless watching Weston inflamed. On the top of the hill, we view buildings and homes on fire. Smoke fills the air so thickly we can smell it on the outskirts of the town. I can hear the yells and screams of people running, but none of this makes sense.

"Andy" Jordan yells pointing to James, Travis, and David coming our way. Looking around for the others I cannot see Rachel's group with them.

Feeling sick I turn towards the boys hoping they aren't in the village. "Where are Rachel and the others" I ask?

"They went on ahead, saying they're going to get food for everyone." James answers looking concerned. I can hear Sarah in the background crying. My heart drops and my worst fears come true.

"When did they leave?" Jacob questions taking charge of the situation.

"They left about an hour ago before the first fires began. We started to get worried after the explosions were heard." David replies looking horrified at the scene. What once was the jewel of the west is being consumed by fire. The smoke alone left a black mass of emptiness in its wake.

People keep filling my mind all at once. Some whom I had known my whole life were in that mayhem. "Oh god. They are down there" Sarah weeps still in a state. At that, a vision comes to me, and everything turns white in a matter of seconds.. I'm swept up so fast I did not have time to prepare.

I find myself at the center of the village filled with happy festival goers. The dancers just finished their performance, and the big show is about to begin. Just as Ariel Matters, the best singer in Weston, gets on stage, I see arrows flying. One of them hits Ariel in the arm as her mother screams, running to her daughter's aid, but the attacks keep coming.

Alek, with what seems to be two hundred men, swarms the festival guards slaughtering them. Tears flowed to my eyes witnessing what happened to the small militia that Weston had assembled.

Watching boys that barely can be called men be overwhelmed and outnumbered is crushing. I recognize one of the men to be Luke, the blacksmith apprentice who teased me in the field. Now he is laying on the ground with a sword in his stomach. The light is gone from his eyes, and his fellow soldiers lay beside him in a similar state.

If only Weston had more resources, then maybe this wouldn't have happened. A shift in my vision occurs directing me from Alek and his men to a newcomer. A man with light brown skin, but I noticed a symbol of the Delianians army on his armor. Dread fills me as I realize the Delianians are finally showing their hands. This is what they were planning the entire time, and now Weston was for the taking. The Delianian must have been a General, as he directed his hundreds of men to reload a weapon. It was made like a cannon but shot fireballs at the buildings as they lit into an inferno. Alek seems overjoyed watching one of the houses burn as innocent people were stuck inside screaming.

Horrified, I scan around to see Malcolm, Louis, and their men captured and led to the marketplace. Breathing a sigh of relief that at least they were alive after seeing so much death so far.

My mind moves again and now I see women and children being held in the center of the square. Seeing the familiar faces of Rachel and Laura in a corner together I thanked the heavens for their safety. Yet my happiness is short lived as I observe something that makes me sick.

My body becomes cold watching my sister and mother not being held hostage. Instead my family members are telling one of the Delianians commanders about Weston's weapons and offering to oversee the villagers. Mel and Ella did nothing as their fellow countrymen died around them.

However my magic wanted to show me they aren't the only traitors Weston had.

I didn't want to see more, but the vision continues. The three Walkers are free now and told the enemy about the escape routes out of the village. Hearing Matthew and Cody celebrate as one of the men who locked them up were tortured is stomach-turning.

Tim, for his part, looks cozy with the Delianians, not surprised at all. My hatred for the Walkers hit an all time high realizing Tim knew this was going to happen. Of course he helped this happen by selling secrets to the enemy. How could people be so heartless; to betray their own home? I keep asking myself this as the dead bodies are being dragged on what used to be the stage. Now the stage was a bonfire to burn the dead and the dying. I identified some of the bodies, especially two of them. Molly and Rebecca the twins from earlier in the day.

I collapse to my knees feeling rocks bite into my skin from the real world. However the images of the girls my age and their bodies being tossed into the fire is still in my mind. "They deserve a proper burial with a service" I cry. Hearing someone call my name, my foresight dissolves and the images of Weston are gone.

Worried green eyes are the first thing I see. Jacob's face is all I need and I crumble again. All the dead villagers in my vision and my family's treachery. It's all too much to handle, and my friends are trapped down there.

"Andy, what did you see?" Jacob urges. Looking up I can see our small group waiting. My mouth is dry, I hated being the one to tell everyone the news. Wiping my face, I stand up and straighten my shoulders.

"Weston was raided." I announce, waiting for the words to hit everyone. The reaction is swift with mutters and gasps from everyone. Searching their faces, I know they're expecting the worst, but an attack isn't on their mind.

"Who raided Weston?" Mark growls, shaking me, as I blink at his closeness.

"The Delianians and Bulkans are the raiders. They defeated Louis and Malcolm's men." I choke out as the others swore. Mark and Jacob look the most affected by the dire news. Both gazes stoned-faced at the village, barely holding in their rage.

"How can this happen? The village should have supplies and defenses planned, so this can't occur." Jacob hisses kicking the hay maze. His frustration is easy to see and what I was about to reveal next wasn't going to help them.

"My mother and sister helped the raiders by revealing the weapons location." I can hear mumbles as my stomach drops, but I have to continue. "The Walkers also helped by revealing Weston's private secrets."

"Of course, this is what Tim Walker must have been doing for months before Louis revealed his schemes." Jacob voices now slightly calmer than before. My fiancé is holding it together well and even squeezes my hand in a way to show support. It feels good knowing he and our friends didn't blame me for my family's deeds.

"What about Rachel?" James asks frantically.

"I saw Rachel and Laura being held hostage in the square with the other women and children." Sighs of relief fill everyone, and I'm happy I am at least able to tell them some good news.

"What about King Louis and Prince Malcolm?" David questions his face going pale.

"Safe as well. They are fine and are being held hostage in the marketplace with the remainder of their men." I answer by thinking of the Weston militia that fought bravely but is sadly gone.

"Brother, we need to flee before they find us missing," Travis speaks. "It's a miracle we are on the outskirts of the village. We should use that to our advantage and escape." Rage and resentment consume me as this boy is willing to run away without our friends.

"You want to abandon Rachel and Laura?" Sarah remarks jumping to her feet just as angry as I am at that moment. Looking at my friend I know the last thing she wants to do is leave. I'm about to tell Travis to go jump in a river when Jacob speaks up.

"We have to leave" he rationalizes and I feel betrayed. I'm about to marry a man who is willing to let my best friends suffer. Feeling myself go numb I shake off his grip and put distance between us.

"I will not leave them to those men." I respond remembering Rebecca's young body being burnt on the stage. "I can't abandon my friends in that place."

" Andy, there is nothing we can do here." Jacob claims trying again to touch me but I flinch away.

"No, they are my friends, I will not go" I shout.

"Then think what they would want for us." Mark declares, grabbing onto my arm tightly and refusing to let go.

"And what would they want Mark?" I hiss glaring at the dark-eyed prince. How dare he say something so absurd to me. I know my friends wouldn't want to be abandoned.

"Rachel and Laura wouldn't want Jordan to be captured, especially in his state" Mark points out. "Going into Weston will put him at risk and without control of his magic, Jordan would most likely be killed."

Those words make Sarah and my resistance vanish. My eyes focus on the small boy who stands by James sucking his thumb staying quiet. Remaining isn't an option for him and his powers. One raw emotion and Jordan will lose control again.

"Andy, we don't make this decision lightly. Jacob and I consider both girls our friends but we have no other choice." Mark states sadly looking back at the village. His expression is troubled and with that, I know he hates this decision as well.

Feeling a touch on my shoulder I come face to face with Jacob's grief-stricken eyes. "I want to help them but it's not possible." Jacob's face makes me ashamed that only seconds ago I thought this man was cold-hearted. I know he loves my friends and has gotten close to Rachel in the past few months. Leaving her was the last thing he wanted to do but Jacob is thinking about everyone's safety, not a few.

With a defeated voice, I know escaping was the best option. "Let's go."

After that decision is made we move quickly to the cornfields that surround the maze. The field is big enough to hide us and it also leads out of the village. One foot after the other is the only thing I'm focused on.

"Andy, we can't go yet, sissy isn't here." Jordan complains beside me as James drags the boy along. I can't answer or even stare at the little boy. He looks so much like Rachel as tears fall from my eyes.

"Jordan, your sister won't mind us leaving." Mark lies picking up Jordan to go faster. With Jordan in Mark's arms the pace increases, and it feels like we ran forever. I thought we had a little farther to be out of Weston, but the sound of rushing water greets us. The West River is in front of us telling us we're out of Weston and decisions need to be made.

"Where do we go from here?" David pants trying to catch his breath.

"The nearest army that can help Louis is in Evergreen. However it's a twenty day journey on foot if we are lucky" I suggest. "The Evergreen's army is formidable and maybe if we went there. Rachel and the others have a chance of being rescued."

"We need that army, it's the largest in this part of the kingdom." Sarah agrees strongly next to me. We both look at our fiancés waiting for their decision.

"Then we must go to Evergreen," Jacob decides. Releasing a sigh, I give a watery smile to Sarah and she returns it. At least this is a small victory for our friend's safety. Finding the route to the port city the others start running again. I am the only one to look back at

Weston one last time. The smoke still clouds the sky and even in the midafternoon it blocks out the sun.

Forcing myself to go forward is necessary as the hours pass. Looking at road markers and counting different wildflowers becomes a game of distraction to me. As the day goes on and dusk approaches we put enough distance between Weston to feel safe. Finding an empty farmhouse, I finally convinced the group to rest for the night.

Sitting on a rock and staring at the direction we came. Laura and Rachel are on my mind. Everything that once was important to me is gone thanks to my mother and sister. My family are traitors, something I wouldn't have thought of them being in my wildest dreams.

"Andy do not worry I am sure Rachel and Laura are fine." Jacob says coming to sit next to me and rubbing my back. I gaze into his green eyes and let myself lay on his shoulders.

"Rachel might be fine, but Alek is still in the village and wants Laura. She isn't safe there" I point out sharing my fears with him. Jacob didn't reassure me this time knowing my words are true and Laura is in danger. Something tells me my instincts were right and my friends are fighting for their lives.

The End of Weston

One day has passed since the invasion of Weston and the fires are nearly gone. The bodies of the dead burning is the only thing left besides survivors. Surrounded by the Delianians and Bulkans, the hostages remained crowded together trying to remain calm. In the corner of the square, Rachel and Laura watch Ella speak to the Delianians general. The man that slaughtered the Weston militia and the royal forces with his mysterious weapon.

"We need to find out if Louis and Malcolm are alive" Laura whispers in tears. Rachel, who is right beside her, feels sympathy for the shorter girl. She just got engaged to the man, and this occurs.

"I think they are in the marketplace. I saw some men being taken in that direction." Rachel answers trying to sound confident but in her own mind. She's a complete mess as memories of Malcolm keep swarming into her brain. She might not have known Malcolm for long but Rachel could tell he was a good man.

"Well good there is still hope." Laura announces wiping her face before scanning the crowd with her unseeing eyes.

" That's right, we still have hope. We'll find a way to escape and find our loved ones." Rachel says with determination.

"I know Rachel, I do not doubt that," Laura says, squeezing her hand. Feeling more reassured Rachel leans in closer as one of the Delianians guards overseeing them glances their way. They both looked down trying to appear unthreatening and less like a troublemaker. Thankfully Andy wasn't here, that girl attracts trouble too easily.

"Gosh, I wish I had brought my knife with me." Laura grunts out messing with the ropes that hold their hands bound. Ella Miller decided that all the women and children should be tied together making it harder for someone to escape.

Scanning the crowd and seeing familiar figures approaching Rachel is worried. However not for herself, but Laura as Alek and Ella come their way. "Be quiet Laura" she warns. "Ella and Alek are coming our way."

Both girls instantly shut their mouths and look at the ground. Ella is the first to speak to the girls in a sickly-sweet manner. Lifting their heads and trying not to glare at the woman they now hated. Ella stands in front of them in a new dress made of silk with a jeweled necklace around her neck. It seems being a traitor is giving her attire an upgrade. "Laura, Alek told me, he is going to make you his wife." She announces looking at Laura waiting for a response, but none come. The silence must have been irksome to the weather witch because she tries again. "Laura, you should be grateful for the offer. A proposal from the General is generous, especially for a girl with your limitations."

Laura to her credit glares at Ella before she finally speaks. "I don't want to speak to a traitor like you." Her words seem to slap the triumph out of Ella's face at being insulted. Andy's mother looks enraged and Rachel moves closer to Laura in case the weather witch attacks her.

"I did what was necessary for Melissa and me to live in luxury." Ella claims, looking at Laura in anger. "We deserve more than to live in this nothing village."

Hearing that Rachel's mouth drops and Laura looks ready to scratch out Ella's eyes.

"These are the people you grew up with, Ella. They thought you were a friend not a traitor." Laura shouts pointing towards the other hostages around them.

"They are the same people that didn't speak up on my behalf when my life was on the line." Ella argues back, glaring at the other hostages." I had nothing left to lose when Alek offered me his deal so I took it." She says not getting any sympathy from the two girls.

Although Laura did seem interested in Ella's deal. "What did the Bulkans promise you for your loyalty?" She asks with curiosity, making Rachel wonder what Laura is thinking.

The gloating air and cockiness appears again on Ella's face. "Melissa will have a castle and live in Bulka. Alek is even willing to let me go with her" she declares in a dreamlike state. "Finally, my daughter and I will have the life we were destined for." Hearing that, Rachel didn't know she could hate someone so much. Of all the selfish things to trade lives for. Ella is genuinely inhuman and Rachel expected Laura to be just as angry but her reaction is the opposite.

Laughing uncontrollably, Laura's small body is shaking. The tone of the laughter wasn't merriment but cruel and calculating Laura is mocking Ella. At her response Ella looks on unamused by the turn of events.

"What's so funny?" She hisses, grabbing Laura's face lifting her up to stand.

If Laura is afraid it wasn't showing as a smirk appears on her face. "You think Alek would honor an agreement with a woman? In his kingdom of Bulka a woman's value is how much their father can sell them for. You've been tricked and don't even know it. " Laura taunts and what she says next in flames Ella. "You are a fool."

The slap comes across Laura's face abruptly knocking the small girl to the ground. Rachel is at her side waiting for the next strike Ella throws at Laura.

"How dare you speak to me like that." Ella tries to say but does not get the chance to finish her words because a sword is thrust into her stomach by Alek. That moment seems to stop everything with Ella turning to the man who just stabbed her.

"Why?" she whimpers weakly, then everything else is a scream when Alek pulls the sword out of her. Stun Ella holds her stomach trying to stop the bleeding. Rachel watches this scene holding Laura too afraid to move.

"A rat like you shouldn't touch my Laura, she is above you." Alek remarks wiping off his sword like Ella's blood is diseased. The uncaring nature of his voice makes Rachel terrified knowing this man did not care about human life.

"I was training her in obedience for your benefit." Ella stammers out with blood soaking her dress now. "I apologize for my error, now please get Laura to heal me before it is too late." The older woman begs only a few minutes from the afterlife without Laura's aid.

"She doesn't need any lessons from a woman that betrayed her Kingdom." Alek says, spitting on Ella's face. "And death at my hand is an honor for a swine like you. So no. Laura isn't permitted to heal you."

Finally realizing that Alek isn't going to aid her. Ella's face has turned red with rage in her last moments. "Alek, you went back on our deal." She accuses taking a pause as the pain gets worse. "You gave your word of my safety and my daughter's."

"We were never going to honor any agreement to a dishonest snake like you." Alek confesses mocking the dying woman before him. Ella's mouth drops, finally realizing Laura's claims were correct and she has been duped.

Her betrayal is laughable, as she speaks in a broken voice. "I was never dishonest to you. Why did you deceive me about Melissa living in a castle."

Alek shakes his head and smirks at Ella. "That part is true." Ella's face shows a small ounce of happiness before Alek snatches it away. " Although your daughter will not be the one to own the castle."

"What do you mean, how can Melissa live in a castle she doesn't own?" Ella questions getting madder at each word. "Melissa is marrying a royal that owns the castle and as the wife it is partially hers."

"I forgot to inform you something important about Bulka Ella. We have no nobles or royalty, so your daughter was never going to be a lady of high nobility." Alek laughs with his men joining him, his humiliation of Ella complete.

"Then what is Melissa's purpose at the castle" Ella asks..

"Ella, she will be a servant to the warlord's wife and his mistresses. The castles in Bulka have lovely servants quarters that your daughter will enjoy. She will clean floors and polish the wife's jewels for the rest of her pitiful life" Alek gloats.

"How dare you deceive me and my daughter after everything we did for you?" Ella screams looking insulted making Rachel snort. The gall of the woman when she did the same thing to Weston. Yet when the roles are reversed, it was a travesty of massive proportions.

"You think we would make that wench of a daughter of yours a Lady." Alek scoffs walking around her like a predator. "She would be lucky to clean a warlord's mistress' gowns."

"Alek, you will pay for this." Ella yells her eyes glowing and a powerful gust of wind knocks Alek and the Delianians general down. The hostages scream, unable to flee the madness around them. "I am going to kill you all for your deceit." Raising her hand to call a storm but whatever was supposed to happen, didn't. An arrow soars through the air and struck her in the throat. Falling down the older witch starts to choke on her own blood.

"Nice shot, Cullen." Alek congratulates the Delianians general on the back as he lowers his weapon. The man in question shrugs off the praise and reattaches the weapon to his back.

"Finally, that annoying woman can remain quiet for good." Cullen announces in the scruffy accent of Aria. Not paying attention to the two men, Rachel and Laura witness Ella's last moment.

Ella in a pool of blood has enough strength to mumble her last words. "Why betray me?"

"Ella, you are a traitor. I witnessed how far your loyalty can last. Why should I trust you? Look at this village that you once called home." Alek says as he gestures to the ruined buildings and homes that were now ashes. His statement hit home as Ella stares at him before passing away.

Observing her death Laura and Rachel can't muster any sympathy for Andy's mother. She not only aided in Weston's destruction but many villagers' deaths as well. To them Ella got exactly what she deserves at the end for her greed.

"Now, that must have been a nasty sight to see for such beautiful young ladies." Cullen declares looking at Laura and Rachel walking up to them. "You are truly a stunning sight, what is your name?" Cullen asks Rachel with lust in his eyes.

"My name is Rachel." She stammers feeling repulsed by the way the man is scanning her body. An urge to soak in a tub of hot water fills her.

"What a pretty name and I am Cullen Taren of Deliania. The son of the tenth heir to the throne" Cullen informs Rachel as she just nods.Lifting her face up as Rachel has to force herself not to cringe or bite off his hand. "I think I will take you back home with me as a mistress." He says touching Rachel's face as she flinches away from his hand.

"Oh, that sounds good, did you hear that Laura. Your friend is going to Deliania and you will be my wife soon." Alek proclaims with Laura quivering. Rachel decides to analyze Cullen to see if he has some weakness to find in case she has to fight him. Cullen has light brown skin and icy blue eyes with a large hook nose. He is at least in his thirties with a muscular form. Rachel's analysis is cut short when screams echo around them. Melissa, upon seeing Ella's dead body let out a shrill of them running to her mother's side.

"What happened to her?" She cries, rocking Ella's dead body back and forth. It's quite a thing to witness with the blond girl desperately trying to wake her deceased mother. Pulling at the arrow lodge in Ella's throat, blood squirts out landing on her face. Ignoring the blood, Melissa continues in vain to wake a dead body.

"It's an easy explanation, I thrust a sword through that rat of a woman but that didn't kill her.After that Cullen here was kind enough to shoot an arrow through her neck ending her miserable life. " Alek answers coldly to the grieving girl.

"Why did you do that to my mother?" Melissa demands with blood on her hands getting up and looking at each man with hate. Her outrage at her mother's killing must be distracting her from Ella's body.

"She attacked us when I told her our deal was false." Alek replies loving how broken Melissa has become. It's like a sick game to him to toy with other's emotions Rachel realizes.

"You promised us that no harm would come to my mother and I. That we could live in a castle in Bulka like royalty for the rest of our lives." Melissa yells out the promises Alek made them..

"Melissa, you inherited your mother's foolishness," laughs Alek. "I didn't promise you that the castle will be yours, dear. The castle will belong to a warlord, and you will be a servant to his wife or mistress." Alek's mockery of Melissa is getting dangerous, as Rachel notices signs of a release of magic coming off the blond witch. Panicking Rachel reaches out for the bloody arrowhead that killed Ella. The blood is cold and sticky but she has a good grip cutting away the ropes that binds her.

"You must pay for killing my mother." Melissa shouts and with a yell the ground begins to shake. Melissa's body glows with a bright dark light making the quake's power increase. The earth split and the buildings around them came crashing down. Freeing herself, Rachel starts on Laura's restraints, cutting them off.

"I will destroy everything" The blond witch roars, sending out waves of magic. Rocks, trees, and animals go into the air pelting people that are defenseless. The hostages desperately all run for cover as Melissa attacks Alek's and Cullen's forces. Her wild burst of power wasn't well directed and most of the casualties were the villagers, not invaders.

People and soldiers flee from the unstable witch as Melissa destroys what is left of the village. Rachel drags Laura to her feet and runs to the marketplace to find the guys. Pushing through panicked people Rachel keeps a tight hold on her small friend not wanting to be separated. Finally making it to their destination all Rachel sees is chaos. Around them are empty booths with hundreds of men tied together as buildings fall around them. Looking to find something to cut their ropes. Rachel sees a sword instantly taking it and running to the nearest man to free him.

"Go free the others and flee" she orders the man. Nodding, he went to help other prisoners as Rachel tried to spot the two people she came to search for. Passing person after person getting desperate as Weston is crumbling around them.

"Rachel, we've got to find them," Laura pleads next to her.

"I know" Rachel says panicking but something red catches her eyes near the remains of the Riverside Inn. There, tied to a post is a heavy-set man with wild auburn hair. "Thank god" she replies, pulling Laura and racing to the man's side. Next to Malcolm is Louis tied to the other side of the post. Both men had minor cuts and bruises but no severe wounds luckily. Rachel weeps freeing them and especially so when Malcolm embraces her.

"Are you alright Laura?" Louis asks, kissing Laura on the mouth.

"Yes Louis, I am." Laura responds by hugging him before smacking him on the head. "No touching before the wedding, what will people say?" Laughing, Louis let go of Laura for a second.

"I am glad you escaped my pretty girl." Malcolm declares, staring at Rachel's amber eyes. "I was sure we were all goners."

Rolling her eyes Rachel snorts, "Malcolm you have a way with words". Bellowing with laughter, the giant's grip on her body loosens but he still holds her close.

"What can I say? Around you I become a sappy fool and poet". Grinning Malcolm leans over Rachel making her feel small for the first time in her life. Being one of the tallest girls in Weston's men always came up short next to her. However with Malcolm Rachel actually feels tiny compared to his massive height.

Just as Rachel sees Malcolm was about to lean in, Laura's voice interrupts them. "Rachel, we need to free everyone before Melissa demolishes the whole village." Jumping at her friend's voice Rachel removes herself from Malcolm. Embarrassed that she got caught up in the moment not seeing the big picture. Looking around there are tons of people that need help and she has to concentrate.

"I guess our reunion will have to wait." Malcolm responds by moving to one of the many men still restrained.

Handing her blade to Malcolm they make quick work of freeing everyone. Once the last man is unbound and untied Louis orders. "We must leave Weston and find other survivors." Saluting soldiers scatter rounding up any civilians still left in the village. Scanning Weston Rachel is in shock at the shape of her once happy home. The earthquake and fires made Weston unrecognizable, bringing tears to her eyes.

It takes an arm around her shoulders from Malcolm to wake her up. He practically drags her along to safety. "We cannot reminisce now Rachel, it's time to go." At his words the tears overflowed from her eyes at her once home. Laura is in a similar state, even if she can't see the destruction around her. Louis takes her hand pulling his fiancée along. "Let's go to the maze. It will be a good spot for a safe zone."

"Good idea" Malcolm agrees, releasing Rachel's hand. After that he starts spreading the word for everyone to meet at the maze. Hearing a horse cry, Rachel races to see a bay horse secured to a fallen tree. Witnessing this she can't leave the frightened beast to its fate. Quickly locating a dagger she releases the horse and leads it to the safe zone. Running now, Rachel coughs from the smoke as she passes the exit of Weston following the others to the maze. Hundreds of civilians and soldiers blend together all heading to the same destination. An urgent concern fills Rachel's heart thinking of her brother and the friends she left behind here.

Once Rachel is at the maze, she begins her search for the others. After an hour she realized they weren't there at the maze. "No, please don't be down there." She prays looking at the village that's now rubble.

"Rachel, they are all right." Laura speaks up suddenly by her side. "The others left the village when the fighting began. I sense Jordan's magic a day west of here. They're heading to Evergreen is my best guess."

"That makes sense, Evergreen has a large army that can help." Louis declares as he and Malcolm come to join them. "I can send a scout to meet our friends, but I need to get back to the capital. The Bulkans and Delianians just declared war. I must prepare."

"I'm going to find them myself" Rachel asserts her mind is already made up. She can't stay here safe knowing her brother is out there afraid. Getting on the bay horse she rescued Rachel is lucky the beast is already saddled.. Just as she's ready to leave a figure blocks her path grabbing her bridle. "Malcolm let go of the rope" She yanks but his grip is unyielding,

"Rachel, you do not know what direction they are going. And besides it's dangerous to leave by yourself" he replies refusing to let her go. Getting mad Rachel's eyes glows preparing to remove Malcolm even by force if needed.

Summoning her magic to do just that, Laura decides to play peacemaker. "I can lead her to Jordan. I have the ability to sense magic so I can track him." Laura offers, getting a horse herself and is up on the beast in seconds.

"Thanks," Rachel says, winking at the Native who only smiles.

"I know you need to be with Jordan. And I need to be with our friends right now."

"You know you two are riding into danger." Malcolm warns but his words aren't convincing the two friends. "Louis talk some sense into them."

Louis thinks for a moment but at the end, he says. "They have the right to go and it isn't any safer here than going out west." Eyeing both, the king gives them both concern stares. "I wish both of you would stay but your friends and families are out there. I'd do the same in your shoes."

"My King, you should go with them to Evergreen." A soldier proposes bowing to Louis, shocking the King.

"I can't leave these people after they lost everything." He answers, pointing at the villagers who are now without a home. The people of Weston have nothing now but the clothes on their back.

"And the Bulkans and Delianians might attack these people again." Malcolm counters back scouting our area.

"The Bulkans and Delianians will not come back for us. There is nothing left of value thanks to my granddaughter. " A remorseful Ruth Miller announces.

Rachel's heart breaks for the old woman watching her home of fifty years be destroyed. Covered with soot and smoke Grandma Ruth didn't seem hurt thankfully. "Grandma, I'm glad you are all right."

"Thanks baby." Ruth smiles a little at Rachel but the sadness in her wrinkled face is easy to see. Melissa and Ella's betrayal struck deep and only time can heal that wound.

"How do you know they won't come back?" Louis asks looking at the elder Miller unconvinced but Laura answers first.

"She is a seer and Andy's grandmother." Laura informs him and with that Louis looks interested at what Ruth has to say.

"I had a vision of them going away and setting up camp a little east of here." Ruth speaks gazing at the ruined remains of the village where they once resided. "It would be foolish to stay. They wanted Weston for its resources and now it has no more. Go King Louis and stop this from happening again to another town."

"Ruth is right, you must go." Mrs. Seymour urges as the other older woman wraps a shawl around Ruth's shoulders.

"King Louis, we can escort the civilians to the nearest village for safekeeping.It's no need for you to come with us." One of the few remaining captains suggested to the king.

Louis shakes his head in disagreement. "It's wrong of me to abandon the Weston villagers."

"You aren't abandoning us but forming a plan. So more villages don't face what Weston dealt with." Andrew Miller asserts limping toward them. Gasping Ruth cries at the state her son appears to be in. Half of Andrew's tanned face is bruised and both of his eyes blackened. His right arm is clearly broken and left leg has been bandaged roughly.

"Mr. Miller, what happened?" Rachel exclaims sliding off of her horse with Laura not far behind them. Ruth and Mrs. Seymour is inspecting the wounds and making room for Laura. Releasing her magic, Laura places her glowing hands on the injured flesh of Andrew..

Wincing at the touch the older redhead explains what happened to him. "I was ambushed when I was at home with Melissa and Ella. Tim and the Bulkans general rammed the door overpowering the guards. I yelled for Melissa and Ella to run but they just stayed put. Even helping those men by using magic to attack us. I watched my daughter cheer on the man that bashed a mallet into my face. Where did I go wrong with that girl." He cries out getting comforted by his mother and Mrs. Seymour.

"Andrew, this isn't your fault. Melissa made her choice." Ruth responds to her son's guilt of Melissa's actions. "You raised her to be a good person like Andy. She chose a different path." Her words hit home as Laura works on healing his wounds, but Andrew stops the Native.

"Save your magic Laura, you have to be ready for a long ride." Frowning at that but she agrees with Andrew after further prodding.

Sighing Louis looks at one of his remaining commanders. "Commander Farris, you're overseeing these people's safety in my absence." The commander nods and with that Louis' men find five extra horses for them and the others.

"Mr. Miller, can you check on my mother and brothers if you see them." Rachel asks, looking around and not seeing any of her family. Dread fills her mind thinking of the chaos of Weston and the real possibility they're gone.

"Rachel, they are fine. I saw them handing out medicine to the wounded." Andrew says in a reassuring tone. Feeling relieved by that news, Rachel realizes that Mr. Miller just lost someone too.

"Mr. Miller, I am sorry about Ella. She's" Rachel starts to say but Laura gives her a hard stare signaling her friend to stay silent.. She can tell the healer believes this is not the time to reveal Ella's death.

Andrew pats her hand not knowing Rachel is keeping a major secret. "I will survive this act of betrayal by Ella, don't worry about me. Go find Andy for me and make sure she's okay." Nodding, Rachel goes over to the horses only to see Malcolm on a huge battle horse coming towards them.

"We need to hurry, it will be dark soon." He states stunning Rachel who is right next to him.

"You are coming too?"

"Yes, I cannot let you three go off without some protection." He jokes earning an eye roll from her.

"We can do without your ego but really why are you not staying with your men."

"They are going with the remaining soldiers to protect the villagers. I feel that I am of better use with you." The grandstanding is gone from his tenor and only sincerity can be heard.

"Thank you Malcolm," Rachel replies, her face blushing. Oh, god she's falling for the Mallorian she groans. After Cody, Rachel promises herself no more men for a long time. And being smitten with another one isn't a good option for her right now. Placing a hand on her stomach Rachel tries not to cry about how stupid she was with Cody. Now she is ruined but Rachel has to focus on getting to Jordan and making sure he is safe.

Shaking her head she gets back on the bay horse. When she is properly secured, does Rachel turn to Laura as their only map? "Laura, please show us the way."

Kicking her horse Laura gallops in the direction that will hopefully take them to their friends. Rachel starts off too, and the men are behind her. All Rachel desired to do was hug her little brother and protect him. That is her job as his big sister and she takes that seriously.

The End.

Thank you

I greatly appreciate all the readers who took the time to read this book. This book has been a frustrating labor of love that I will never forget. If you like the book please leave a review as a self published author feedback and support is greatly needed.

Please stay tuned for the next book in the series "The Witches of Weston is ready for reading.

Books by Dominique Pryor
The Royal Magic Series

Royal Magic Book 1
The Witches of Witches Book 2
The Trials of Earth Witch Book 3
Coming soon 2024
Sarah's story Book 4

Books I highly recommend to read for all fiction lovers.

Fire Mage by Trudi Jaye
The Dark Amulet series by Jennifer Ealey
Steelflower by Lilth Saintcrow
William of Alamore Series by C.J R Isely